Praise for

ANNIE ON MY MIND

"The story of two young women who love each other.
It is an honest portrayal of their love with an ending
that is in keeping with, and worthy of, the rest of
the book."   —*The Baltimore Sun*

"*Annie on My Mind* was an eye-opener (maybe 'heart-
opener' is a better term)."
                              —*The Milwaukee Journal*

"A tender, bittersweet love story."
                    —Young Adult Reviewers' Choice/*Booklist*

"Departs from the fact-packed preachiness of the
problem novel to become instead a compelling story
of two real and intriguing young women. There have
been many books for teenagers, fiction and nonfic-
tion, that give lots of useful and accurate information about homosexuality; here's one that tells *what
it feels like*, one that has, finally, romance."
                    —STARRED/*School Library Journal*

An ALA Best of the Best Books for Young Adults

Also by Nancy Garden

*Hear Us Out! Lesbian and Gay Stories of Struggle, Progress,
and Hope, 1950 to the Present*
Prisoner of Vampires
Peace, O River
What Happened in Marston
Berlin: City Split in Two
The Loners
Vampires
Werewolves
Witches
Devils and Demons
The Kids' Code and Cipher Book
Lark in the Morning
Meeting Melanie
My Sister, the Vampire
My Brother, the Werewolf
Dove and Sword
Good Moon Rising
The Year They Burned the Books
The Case of the Stolen Scarab
Endgame
Holly's Secret

The Fours Crossing Books
Fours Crossing
Watersmeet
The Door Between

The Monster Hunters Series
Mystery of the Night Raiders
Mystery of the Midnight Menace
Mystery of the Secret Marks
Mystery of the Kidnapped Kidnapper
Mystery of the Watchful Witches

Molly's Family
(Pictures by Sharon Wooding)

ANNIE
ON MY
MIND

Nancy Garden

Includes an interview with the author
conducted by Kathleen T. Horning

SQUARE FISH

FARRAR STRAUS GIROUX
NEW YORK

*This story is not true. The characters are fictitious
and there is no Foster Academy in real life. The house
shared by Ms. Stevenson and Ms. Widmer bears a strong
resemblance to a house I once lived in and loved dearly;
however, to the best of my knowledge, no incident like the one
described in this book ever took place there.*

NANCY GARDEN

SQUARE
FISH

An imprint of Macmillan Publishing Group, LLC
120 Broadway
New York, NY 10271
fiercereads.com

Library of Congress Cataloging-in-Publication Data
Garden, Nancy.
   Annie on my mind / Nancy Garden.
      p.   cm.
   Summary: Liza puts aside her feelings for Annie after the disaster at school,
but eventually she allows love to triumph over the ignorance of people.
      ISBN 978-0-374-40011-8
      [1. Lesbians—Fiction.] I. Title.
   PZ7.G165 An 1982   [Fic]—dc19   82-09189

Originally published in the United States by Farrar Straus Giroux
First Square Fish Edition: February 2013
Square Fish logo designed by Filomena Tuosto

30 29 28 27 26 25 24 23 22

AR: 6.0 / LEXILE: 1000L

For all of us

ANNIE ON MY MIND

It's raining, Annie.

Liza—Eliza Winthrop—stared in surprise at the words she'd just written; it was as if they had appeared without her bidding on the page before her. "Frank Lloyd Wright's house at Bear Run, Pennsylvania," she had meant to write, "is one of the earliest and finest examples of an architect's use of natural materials and surroundings to . . ."

But the gray November rain splashed insistently against the window of her small dormitory room, its huge drops shattering against the glass as the wind blew.

Liza turned to a fresh page in her notebook and wrote:

Dear Annie,
It's raining, raining the way it did when I met you last November, drops so big they run together in ribbons, remember?
Annie, are you all right?
Are you happy, did you find what you wanted to find in California? Are you singing? You must be, but you haven't said so in your letters. Do other people get goose-bumps when you sing, the way I used to?
Annie, the other day I saw a woman who reminded

3

*me of your grandmother, and I thought of you, and your
room, and the cats, and your father telling stories in his
cab when we went for that drive on Thanksgiving. Then
your last letter came, saying you're not going to write
any more till you hear from me.*

*It's true I haven't written since the second week you
were in music camp this summer. The trouble is that
I kept thinking about what happened—thinking around
it, really—and I couldn't write you. I'm sorry. I know
it's not fair. It's especially not fair because your letters have
been wonderful, and I know I'm going to miss them. But
I don't blame you for not writing any more, really I don't.*

*Annie, I still can't write, I guess, for I already know
I'm not going to mail this.*

Liza closed her eyes, absently running her hand through
her short, already tousled brownish hair. Her shoulders
were hunched tensely in a way that made her look, even
when she stood up, shorter than the 5'3" she really was.
She moved her shoulders forward, then back, in an un-
conscious attempt to ease the ache that had come from
sitting too long at her drawing board and afterwards at her
desk. The girl who lived across the hall teased her for being a perfectionist, but since many of the other freshman
architecture students had arrived at MIT—Massachusetts
Institute of Technology—fresh from summer internships
with large firms, Liza had spent her first weeks trying dog-
gedly to catch up.

Even so, there was still an unfinished floor plan on her
drawing board, and the unfinished Frank Lloyd Wright
paper on her desk.

4

Liza put down her pen, but in a few moments picked it up again.

What I have to do, I think, before I can mail you a letter, is sort out what happened. I have to work through it all again—everything—the bad parts, but the good ones too—us and the house and Ms. Stevenson and Ms. Widmer, and Sally and Walt, and Ms. Baxter and Mrs. Poindexter and the trustees, and my parents and poor bewildered Chad. Annie—there are things I'm going to have to work hard at remembering.

But I do want to remember, Liza thought, going to her window. I do want to, now.

The rain hid the Charles River and most of the campus; she could barely see the building opposite hers. She looked across at it nonetheless, willing it to blur into— what? Her street in Brooklyn Heights, New York, where she'd lived all her life till now? Her old school, Foster Academy, a few blocks away from her parents' apartment? Annie's street in Manhattan; Annie's school? Annie herself, as she'd looked that first November day . . .

1

Ms. Widmer, who taught English at Foster Academy, always said that the best way to begin a story is to start with the first important or exciting incident and then fill in the background.

So I'm going to start with the rainy Sunday last November when I met Annie Kenyon. I've wanted to be an architect since long before I could spell the word, so I've always spent a lot of time at museums. That day, to help focus my ideas for the solar house I was designing for my senior project, I went to the Metropolitan Museum of Art, to visit the Temple of Dendur and the American Wing.

The museum was so full of people I decided to start with the American Wing, because it's sometimes less crowded, especially up on the third floor where I wanted to go. And at first it seemed as if that was going to be true. When I got to the top of the stairs, everything was so quiet that I thought there might even be no one there at all— but as I started walking toward the colonial rooms, I heard someone singing. I remember I stood and listened for a minute and then went toward the sound, mostly out of curiosity, but also because whoever it was had a wonderful voice.

There was a girl about my age—seventeen—sitting at

a window in one of the oldest colonial rooms, singing and gazing outside. Even though I knew that the only thing outside that window was a painted backdrop, there was something about the girl, the gray cape she was wearing, and the song she was singing, that made it easy to imagine "Plimoth" Plantation or Massachusetts Bay Colony outside instead. The girl looked as if she could have been a young colonial woman, and her song seemed sad, at least the feeling behind it did; I didn't pay much attention to the words.

After a moment or two, the girl stopped singing, although she still kept looking out the window.

"Don't stop," I heard myself saying. "Please."

The girl jumped as if my voice had frightened her, and she turned around. She had very long black hair, and a round face with a small little-kid's nose and a sad-looking mouth—but it was her eyes I noticed most. They were as black as her hair and they looked as if there was more behind them than another person could possibly ever know.

"Oh," she said, putting her hand to her throat—it was a surprisingly long, slender hand, in contrast to the roundness of her face. "You startled me! I didn't know anyone was there." She pulled her cape more closely around her.

"It was beautiful, the singing," I said quickly, before I could feel self-conscious. I smiled at her; she smiled back, tentatively, as if she were still getting over being startled. "I don't know what that song was, but it sounded just like something someone would have sung in this room."

The girl's smile deepened and her eyes sparkled for just a second. "Oh, do you really think so?" she said. "It wasn't a real song—I was just making it up as I went along. I was pretending that I was a colonial girl who missed England —you know, her best friend, things like that. And her dog—she'd been allowed to take her cat but not her dog." She laughed. "I think the dog's name was something terribly original like Spot."

I laughed, too, and then I couldn't think of anything more to say.

The girl walked to the door as if she were going to leave, so I quickly said, "Do you come here often?" Immediately I felt myself cringe at how dumb it sounded.

She didn't seem to think it was dumb. She shook her head as if it were a serious question and said, "No. I have to spend a lot of time practicing, only that gets dull sometimes." She tossed her hair back over the shoulder of her cape. The cape fell open a little and I could see that under it she was wearing a very uncolonial pair of green corduroy jeans and a brown sweater.

"Practicing?" I asked. "Singing, you mean?"

She nodded and said in an offhand way, "I'm in this special group at school. We keep having to give recitals. Do you come here often?" She was standing fairly close to me now, leaning against the door frame, her head tipped a little to one side.

I told her I did and explained about wanting to be an architect and about the solar house. When I said I was going to the Temple of Dendur, she said she'd never seen it except from outside the museum, and asked, "Mind if I come?"

I was surprised to find that I didn't; I usually like to be

by myself in museums, especially when I'm working on something. "No," I said. "Okay—I mean, no, I don't mind."

We walked all the way downstairs, me feeling kind of awkward, before I had the sense to say, "What's your name?"

"Annie Kenyon," she said. "What . . . what's that?"

I said "Liza Winthrop" before I realized that wasn't what she'd asked. We'd just gotten to the medieval art section, which is a big open room with a magnificent choir screen—an enormous gold-painted wrought-iron grating—running across the whole back section. Annie stood in front of it, her eyes very bright.

"It's from a Spanish cathedral," I said, showing off. "1668 . . ."

"It's beautiful," Annie interrupted. She stood there silently, as if in awe of the screen, and then bowed her head. Two or three people coming in glanced at her curiously and I tried to tell myself it was ridiculous for me to feel uneasy. *You could walk away,* I remember thinking; *you don't know this person at all. Maybe she's crazy. Maybe she's some kind of religious fanatic.*

But I didn't walk away, and in a couple of seconds she turned, smiling. "I'm sorry," she said as we left the room, "if I embarrassed you."

"That's okay," I said.

Even so, I led Annie fairly quickly to the Hall of Arms and Armor, which I usually go through on my way to the temple. The Hall is one of my favorite parts of the museum—one is greeted at its door by a life-sized procession of knights in full armor, on horseback. The first knight has his lance at the ready, pointed straight ahead, which means right at whoever walks in.

Annie seemed to love it. I think that's one of the first things that made me decide I really did like her, even though she seemed a little strange. "Oh—*look!*" she exclaimed, walking around the procession. "Oh—they're wonderful!" She walked faster, flourishing an imaginary lance, and then began prancing as if she were on horseback herself.

Part of me wanted to join in; as I said, I've always loved those knights myself, and besides, I'd been a King Arthur nut when I was little. But the other part of me was stiff with embarrassment. "Annie," I began, in the warning voice my mother used to use when my brother and I got too exuberant as children. But by then Annie had pretended to fall off her horse, dropping her lance. She drew an imaginary sword so convincingly I knew I was admiring her skill in spite of myself, and then when she cried, *"En garde! Stand and fight or I'll run you through!"* I knew I wasn't going to be able to keep from smiling much longer. "If you do not fight me, knight," she said, "you will rue the day that ever you unhorsed me here in this green wood!"

I had to laugh then, her mood was so catching. Besides, by then I'd noticed that the only other people around were a couple of little boys at the opposite end of the Hall. In the next minute I completely stopped resisting. I imagined a horse and leapt down from it, crying in my best King Arthur style, "I will not fight an unhorsed knight and me mounted. But now that I am on the ground, you will not live to tell the tale of this day's battle!" I pretended to throw aside my lance and draw a sword, too.

"Nor you!" cried Annie with a lack of logic that we laughed about later. "Have at you, then!" she shouted, swiping at me with her sword.

In another minute we were both hopping in and out of the procession of knights, laying about with our imaginary swords and shouting chivalrous insults at each other. After about the third insult, the little boys left the other end of the Hall and came over to watch us.

"I'm for the one in the cape!" one of them shouted. "Go, Cape!"

"I'm not," said his friend. "Go, Raincoat!"

Annie and I caught each other's eyes and I realized that we were making a silent agreement to fight on till the death for the benefit of our audience. The only trouble was, I wasn't sure how we were going to signal each other which one of us was going to die and when.

"Here—what's going on here? Stop that, you two, this instant—old enough to know better, aren't you?" I felt a strong hand close around my shoulder and I turned and saw the uniform of a museum guard topped by a very red, very angry face.

"We're terribly sorry, sir," Annie said, with a look of such innocence I didn't see how anyone could possibly be angry at her. "The knights are so—so splendid! I've never seen them before—I got carried away."

"Harrumph!" the guard said, loosening his hold on my shoulder and saying again, "Old enough to know better, both of you." He glared at the two little boys, who by now were huddled together, mouths wide open. "Don't let this give you any ideas," he roared after them as they scurried off like a pair of frightened field mice. When they were gone, the guard scowled at us again—his forehead scowled, that is, but his eyes didn't look angry. "Darn good fight," he grunted. "Ought to do Shakespeare in the Park, you two. But no more," he said, shaking his finger. "Not here—understand?"

"Oh, yes, sir," Annie said contritely, and I nodded, and we stood there practically holding our breaths as he lumbered away. The second he was gone, we both burst out laughing.

"Oh, Liza," Annie said, "I don't know when I've had so much fun."

"Neither do I," I said truthfully. "And, hey, guess what? I wasn't even embarrassed, except right at the beginning."

Then a funny thing happened. We looked at each other, really looked, I mean, for the first time, and for a moment or two I don't think I could have told anyone my name, let alone where I was. Nothing like that had ever happened to me before, and I think—I know—it scared me.

It was a bit longer before I could speak, and even then all I could say was, "Come on—the temple's this way."

We went silently through the Egyptian section, and I watched Annie's face as we walked into the Sackler Wing and she saw the Temple of Dendur, with the pool and open space in front of it. It's a sight that stuns most people, and it still stuns me, even though I've been there many times. It's the absence of shadows, I think, and the brightness— stark and pure, even on a day as rainy as that one was. Light streams in through glass panels that are as open as the sky and reflects from the pool, making the temple's present setting seem as vast and changeable as its original

13

one on the river Nile must have been thousands of years ago.

Annie gasped as soon as we walked in. "It's outdoors!" she said. "Like it, I mean. But—but exactly like it." She threw out her arms as if embracing all of it, and let out her breath in an exasperated sigh, as if she were frustrated at not being able to find the right words.

"I know," I said; I'd never felt I'd found the right words, either—and Annie smiled. Then, her back very straight, she walked slowly around the pool and up to the temple as if she were the goddess Isis herself, inspecting it for the first time and approving.

When she came back, she stood so close to me our hands would have touched if we'd moved them. "Thank you," she said softly, "for showing me this. The choir screen, too." She stepped back a little. "This room seems like you." She smiled. "Bright and clear. Not somber like me and the choir screen."

"But you're . . ." I stopped, realizing I was about to say *beautiful*—surprised at thinking it, and confused again.

Annie's smile deepened as if she'd heard my thought, but then she turned away. "I should go," she said. "It's getting late."

"Where do you live?" The words slipped out before I could think much about them. But there didn't seem any reason not to ask.

"Way uptown," Annie said, after hesitating a moment. "Here . . ." She pushed her cape back and groped in a pocket, pulling out a pencil stub and a little notebook. She scribbled her address and phone number, tore the page off, and handed it to me. "Now you have to give me yours."

I did, and then we just sort of chatted as we walked back through the Egyptian section and outside into the rain. I don't remember what we said; but I do remember feeling that something important had happened, and that words didn't matter much.

In a few more minutes, Annie was on a crosstown bus, and I was heading in the opposite direction to get the IRT subway home to Brooklyn. I was halfway home before I realized I hadn't done any thinking about my solar-house project at all.

2

The next day, Monday, was warm, more like October than November, and I was surprised to see that there were still leaves left on the trees after the rain the day before. The leaves on the street were almost dry, at least the top layer of them, and my brother Chad and I shuffled through them as we walked to school. Chad's two years younger than I, and he's supposed to look like me: short, square, and blue-eyed, with what Mom calls a "heart-shaped face."

About three years after Mom and Dad were married, they moved from Cambridge, Massachusetts, where MIT is, to Brooklyn Heights, just across from lower Manhattan. The Heights isn't at all like Manhattan, the part of New York that most people visit—in many ways it's more like a town than a city. It has more trees and flowers and bushes than Manhattan, and it doesn't have lots of big fancy stores, or vast office buildings, or the same bustling atmosphere. Most of the buildings in the Heights are residential—four- or five-story brownstones with little back and front gardens. I've always liked living there, although it does have a tendency to be a bit dull in that nearly everyone is white, and most people's parents have jobs as doctors, lawyers, professors—or VIP's in brokerage firms, publishing houses, or the advertising business.

Anyway, as Chad and I shuffled through the leaves to school that Monday morning, Chad was muttering the Powers of Congress and I was thinking about Annie. I wondered if I'd hear from her and if I'd have the nerve to call her if I didn't. I had put the scrap of paper with her address on it in the corner of my mirror where I would see it whenever I had to brush my hair, so I thought I probably would call her if she didn't call me first.

Chad tugged my arm; he looked annoyed—no, exasperated.

"Huh?" I said.

"Where are you, Liza? I just went through the whole list of the Powers of Congress and then asked you if it was right and you didn't even say anything."

"Good grief, Chad, I don't remember the whole list."

"I don't see why not, you always get A's in everything. What's the point of learning something sophomore year if you're only going to forget it by the time you're a senior?" He shoved his hair back in the way that usually makes Dad say he needs a haircut, and picked up a double handful of leaves, cascading them over my head and grinning— Chad's never been able to stay mad at anyone very long. "You must be in love or something, Lize," he said, using the one-syllable nickname he has for me. Then he went back to my real name and chanted, "Liza's in love, Liza's in love . . ."

Funny, that he said that.

By then we were almost at school, but I slung my book bag over my shoulder and pelted him with leaves the rest of the way to the door.

Foster Academy looks like an old wooden Victorian

mansion, which is exactly what it was before it was made into an independent—private—school running from kindergarten through twelfth grade. Some of the turrets and gingerbready decorations on its dingy white main building had begun to crumble away since I'd been in Upper School (high school), and each year more kids had left to go to public school. Since most of Foster's money came from tuition and there were only about thirty kids per class, losing more than a couple of students a year was a major disaster. So that fall the Board of Trustees had consulted a professional fund raiser who had helped "launch" a "major campaign," as Mrs. Poindexter, the headmistress, was fond of saying. By November, the parents' publicity committee had put posters all over the Heights asking people to give money to help the school survive, and there were regular newspaper ads, and plans for a student recruitment drive in the spring. As a matter of fact, when I threw my last handful of leaves at Chad that morning, I almost hit the publicity chairman for the fund drive instead—Mr. Piccolo, father of one of the freshmen.

I said, "Good morning, Mr. Piccolo," quickly, to cover what I'd done.

He nodded and gave us both a kind of ostrichy smile. Like his daughter Jennifer, he was tall and thin, and I could see Chad pretending to play a tune as he went down the hall. It was a school joke that both Mr. Piccolo and Jennifer looked like the musical instrument they were named for.

I grinned, making piccolo-playing motions back to Chad, and then threaded my way down to my locker through knots of kids talking about their weekends. But even

though I said hi to a couple of people, I must still have
been pretty preoccupied because I found out later I'd
walked right past a large red-lettered sign on the basement
bulletin board, next to the latest fund-raising poster—
walked right past it without seeing it at all:

SALLY JARRELL'S EAR PIERCING CLINIC
NOON TO ONE, MONDAY, NOVEMBER 15
BASEMENT GIRLS' ROOM
$1.50 per hole per ear

Sally Jarrell was at that point just about my favorite
person at school. We were as different from each other as
two people can be—I think the main thing we had in com-
mon was that neither of us quite fit in at Foster. I don't
want to say that Foster is snobby, because that's what people always think about private schools, but I guess it's true
that a lot of kids thought they were pretty special. And
there were a lot of cliques, only Sally and I weren't in any
of them. The thing I liked best about her, until everything changed, was that she always went her own way. In
a world of people who seemed to have come out of dupli-
cating machines, Sally Jarrell was no one's copy, not that
fall anyway.

I swear I didn't notice the sign even when I walked
past it a second time—and that time Sally was right in
front of it, peering at my left ear as if there were a bug on
it, and murmuring something that sounded like "posts."
All I noticed was that Sally's thin and rather wan face
looked a little thinner and wanner than usual, probably
because she hadn't had time to wash her hair—it was

hanging around her shoulders in lank strings. "Definitely posts," she said.

That time I heard her clearly, but before I could ask her what she was talking about, the first bell rang and the hall suddenly filled with sharp elbows and the din of banging lockers. I went to chemistry, and Sally flounced mysteriously off to gym. And I forgot the whole thing till lunchtime, when I went back down to my locker for my physics book—I was taking a heavy science load that year because of wanting to go to MIT.

The basement hall was three deep with girls, looking as if they were lined up for something. There were a few boys, too, standing near Sally's boyfriend, Walt, who was next to a table with a white cloth on it. Neatly arranged on the cloth were a bottle of alcohol, a bowl of ice, a spool of white thread, a package of needles, and two halves of a raw potato, peeled.

"Hey, Walt," I asked, mystified, "what's going on?"

Walt, who was kind of flashy—"two-faced," Chad called him, but I liked him—grinned and pointed with a flourish to the poster. "One-fifty per hole per ear," he read cheerfully. "One or two, Madame President? Three or four?"

The reason he called me Madame President was the same reason I was standing there staring at the poster, wishing I were home sick in bed with the flu. I've never quite figured out why, but at election time, one of the kids in my class had nominated me for student-council president, and I'd won. Student council, representing the student body, was supposed to run the school, instead of the faculty or the administration running it. As far as I was concerned, my main responsibility as council president was to preside at meetings every other week. But Mrs. Poindexter, the headmistress, had other ideas. Back in September, she'd given me an embarrassing lecture about setting an example and being her "good right hand" and making sure everyone followed "both the spirit and the letter" of the school rules, some of which were a little screwy.

"Step right up," Walt was shouting. "If the gracious president of student council—of our entire august student body, I might add—will set the trend"—he bowed to me —"business will be sure to boom. Do step this way, Madame . . ."

"Oh, shut up, Walt," I said, trying to run through the school rules in my mind and hoping I wouldn't come up with one that Mrs. Poindexter might think applied specifically to ear piercing.

Walt shrugged, putting his hand under my elbow and ushering me to the head of the line. "At least, Madame President," he said, "let me invite you to observe."

I thought about saying no, but decided it would probably make sense for me to get an idea of what was going on, so I nodded. Walt shot the cuffs of his blue shirt—he was a very snappy dresser, and that day he was wearing a tan three-piece suit—and bowed. "One moment, ladies and gentlemen," he said, "while I escort the president on a tour of the—er—establishment. I shall return." He steered me toward the door and then turned, winking at the few boys who were clustered around the table. "Ms.

Jarrell told me she would take care of you gentlemen after she has—er—accommodated a few of the ladies." He poked Chuck Belasco, who was captain of the football team, in the ribs as we went by and murmured, "She also said to tell you guys she's looking forward to it." That, of course, led to a lot of gruff laughter from the boys.

I went into the girls' room just in time to hear Jennifer Piccolo squeal "Ouch!" and to see tears filling her big brown eyes.

I closed the door quickly—Chuck was trying to peer in —and worked my way through the five or six girls standing around the table Sally had set up in front of the row of sinks. It had the same stuff on it that the one in the hall did.

"Hi, Liza," Sally said cheerfully. "Glad you dropped in." Sally had on a white lab coat and was holding half a potato in one hand and a bloody needle in the other.

"What happened?" I asked, nodding toward Jennifer, who was sniffing loudly as she delicately fingered the pinkish thread that dangled from her right ear.

Sally shrugged. "Low pain threshold, I guess. Ready for the next one, Jen?"

Jennifer nodded bravely and closed her eyes while Sally threaded the bloody needle and wiped it off with alcohol, saying, "See, Liza, perfectly sanitary." The somewhat apprehensive group of girls leaned sympathetically toward Jennifer as Sally approached her right ear again.

"Sally . . ." I began, but Jennifer interrupted.

"Maybe," she said timidly, just as Sally positioned the half potato behind her ear—to keep the needle from going through to her head if it slipped, I realized, shudder-

22

ing—"I'd rather just have one hole in each ear, okay?" She opened her eyes and looked hopefully at Sally.

"You said two holes in two ears," Sally said firmly. "Four holes in all."

"Yes, but—I just remembered my mother said something the other day about two earrings in one ear looking dumb, and I—well, I just wonder if maybe she's right, that's all."

Sally sighed and moved around to Jennifer's other ear. "Ice, please," she said.

Four kids reached for the ice while Jennifer closed her eyes again, looking more or less like my idea of what Joan of Arc must have looked like on her way to the stake.

I'm not going to describe the whole process, mostly because it was a bit gory, but even though Jennifer gave a sort of squeak when the needle went in, and even though she reeled dizzily out of the girls' room (scattering most of the boys, Walt said afterwards), she insisted it hadn't hurt much.

I stayed long enough to see that Sally was trying to be careful, given the limits of her equipment. The potato really did prevent the needle from going too far, and the ice, which was for numbing the ear, did seem to reduce both the pain and the bleeding. Sally even sterilized the ear as well as the needle and thread. The whole thing looked pretty safe, and so I decided that all I had to do in my official capacity was remind Sally to use the alcohol each time.

But that afternoon there were a great many bloody Kleenexes being held to earlobes in various classes, and right after the last bell, when I was standing in the hall

23

talking to Ms. Stevenson, who taught art and was also faculty adviser to student council, a breathless freshman came running up and said, "Oh, good, Liza, you're still here. Mrs. Poindexter wants to see you."

"Oh?" I said, trying to sound casual. "What about?"

Ms. Stevenson raised her eyebrows. Ms. Stevenson was very tall and pale, with blond hair that she usually wore in a not-terribly-neat pageboy. My father always called her the "Renaissance woman," because besides teaching art she coached the debate team, sang in a community chorus, and tutored kids in just about any subject if they were sick for a long time. She also had a fierce temper, but along with that went a reputation for being fair, so no one minded very much, at least not among the kids.

I tried to ignore Ms. Stevenson's raised eyebrows and concentrate on the freshman.

"I don't really know what she wants," the freshman was saying, "but I think it has something to do with Jennifer Piccolo because I saw Mr. Piccolo and Jennifer come out of the nurse's office and then go into Mrs. Poindexter's, and Jennifer was crying and her ears were all bloody." The freshman giggled.

When she left, Ms. Stevenson turned to me and said dryly, "Your ears, I'm glad to see, look the same as ever."

I glanced pointedly at Ms. Stevenson's small silver post earrings.

"Oh, those," she said. "Yes, my doctor pierced my ears when I was in college. My *doctor*, Liza."

I started to walk away.

"Liza, it *was* foolish, Sally's project. I wish I'd known about it in time to stop it."

My feet were heavy as I went down the hall to Mrs. Poindexter's office. I knew that Ms. Stevenson, even though she never made herself obnoxious about it, was usually right. And by the time the whole thing was over with, I wished she'd known about the ear piercing in time to stop it, too.

3

Mrs. Poindexter didn't look up when I went into her office. She was a stubby gray-haired woman who wore rimless glasses on a chain and always looked as if she had a pain somewhere. Maybe she always did, because often when she was thinking up one of her sardonically icy things to say she'd flip her glasses down onto her bumpy bosom and pinch her nose as if her sinuses hurt her. But I always had the feeling that what she was trying to convey was that the student she was disciplining was what really gave her the pain. She could have saved herself a lot of trouble by following the school charter: "The Administration of Foster Academy shall *guide* the students, but the students shall *govern* themselves." But I guess she was what Mr. Jorrocks, our American history teacher, would call a "loose constructionist," because she interpreted the charter differently from most people.

"Sit down, Eliza," Mrs. Poindexter said, still not looking up. Her voice sounded tired and muffled—as if her mouth were full of gravel.

I sat down. It was always hard not to be depressed in Mrs. Poindexter's office, even if you were there to be congratulated for winning a scholarship or making straight A's. Mrs. Poindexter's love for Foster, which was considerable, didn't inspire her to do much redecorating. Her office was in shades of what seemed to be its original brown, without anything for contrast, not even plants, and she kept her thick brown drapes partway closed, so it was unusually dark.

Finally Mrs. Poindexter raised her head from the folder she was thumbing through, flipped her glasses onto her chest, pinched her nose, and looked at me as if she thought I had the personal moral code of a sea slug. "Eliza Winthrop," she said, regret sifting through the gravel in her mouth, "I do not know how to tell you how deeply shocked I am at your failure to do your duty not only as head of student council and therefore my right hand, but also simply as a member of the student body. Words fail me," she said—but, like most people who say that, she somehow managed to continue. "The reporting rule, Eliza—can it be that you have forgotten the reporting rule?"

I felt as if I'd swallowed a box of the little metal sinkers my father uses when he goes fishing in the country. "No," I said, only it came out more like a bleat than a word.

"No, what?"

"No, Mrs. Poindexter."

"Kindly recite the rule to me," she said, closing her eyes and pinching her nose.

I cleared my throat, telling myself she couldn't possibly expect me to remember it word for word as it appeared in the little blue book called *Welcome to Foster Academy*.

"The reporting rule," I began. "One: If a student breaks a rule he or she is supposed to report himself or herself by writing his or her name and what rule he or she has broken

27

on a piece of paper and putting it into the box next to Ms. Baxter's desk in the office."

Ms. Baxter was a chirpy little birdlike woman with dyed red hair who taught The Bible as Literature to juniors and told Bible stories to the Lower School once a week. Her other job was to be Mrs. Poindexter's administrative assistant, which meant Mrs. Poindexter confided in her and gave her special jobs, anything from pouring tea at Mothers Club meetings to doing confidential typing and guarding the reporting box. Ms. Baxter and Mrs. Poindexter drank tea together every afternoon out of fancy Dresden china cups, but they never seemed quite like equals, the way real friends are. They were more like an eagle and a sparrow, or a whale and its pilot fish, because Ms. Baxter was always scurrying around running errands for Mrs. Poindexter or protecting her from visitors she didn't want to see.

"Go on," said Mrs. Poindexter.

"Two," I said. "If a student sees another student breaking a rule, that student is supposed to ask the one who broke the rule to report himself. Or herself. Three: If the student won't do that, the one who saw him or her break the rule is supposed to report them, the one breaking the rule, I mean."

Mrs. Poindexter nodded. "Can you tell me," she said, without opening her eyes, "since you seem to know the rule so well, and since you are well aware that the spirit behind all Foster's rules encompasses the idea of not doing harm to others, why you did not ask Sally Jarrell to report herself when you saw what she was planning to do? Or when you saw what she was actually doing?"

Before I could answer, Mrs. Poindexter whirled around in her chair and opened her eyes, flashing them at me. "Eliza, you should be more aware than most students, given your position, that this school is in desperate need of money and therefore in desperate need of Mr. Piccolo's services as publicity chairman of our campaign. And yet Jennifer Piccolo had to go home early this afternoon because of the terrible pain in her earlobes."

"I'm really sorry, Mrs. Poindexter," I said, and then tried to explain that I hadn't even noticed Sally's sign till she was already piercing Jennifer's ears.

She shook her head as if she couldn't quite grasp that. "Eliza," she said tiredly, "you know that I thought it unwise last spring when you said in your campaign speech that you were against the reporting rule . . ."

"Everyone's against it," I said, which was true—even the faculty agreed that it didn't work.

"Not quite everyone," said Mrs. Poindexter. "Popular or not, that rule is the backbone of this school's honor system, and has been for many, many years—ever since Letitia Foster founded the school, in fact. Not," she added, "that the reporting rule or any other rule will make any difference at all if Foster has to close."

I studied her face, trying to figure out if she was exaggerating. The idea of Foster's having to close had never occurred to me, although of course I knew about the financial troubles. But having to close? Both Chad and I had gone to Foster since kindergarten; it was almost another parent to us. "I—I didn't realize things were that bad," I sputtered.

Mrs. Poindexter nodded. "If the campaign is unsuccessful," she said, "Foster may well have to close. And if Mr. Piccolo, without whose publicity there can be no campaign, leaves us as a result of this—this foolish, thoughtless incident, I seriously doubt we will find anyone to replace him. If he leaves, goodness knows whether the fund raiser who has agreed to act as consultant will stay on—it was hard enough getting both of them in the first place . . ." Mrs. Poindexter closed her eyes again, and for the first time since I'd walked into her office that afternoon I realized she really was upset; she wasn't just acting that way for effect, the way she usually seemed to be. "How do you think Mr. Piccolo will feel about asking people for money now?" she said. "How do you think he will feel about publicizing a school—asking parents to enroll their sons and daughters in a school—where discipline is so lax it cannot prevent its students from doing physical harm to one another?"

"I don't know, Mrs. Poindexter," I said, trying not to squirm. "Pretty bad, I guess."

Mrs. Poindexter sighed. "I would like you to think about all of this, Eliza," she said. "And about the extent of your responsibility to Foster, between now and this Friday's student council meeting. We will hold a disciplinary hearing for you and for Sally Jarrell at that time. Naturally, I cannot allow you to preside, since you are under a disciplinary cloud yourself. I will ask Angela Cariatid, as vice president, to take the gavel. Now you may go."

The leaves that had seemed so crisp that morning looked tired and limp as I walked slowly home without Chad, who had soccer practice, and the sky was lowering again, as if we were going to get more rain.

I was glad Chad wasn't with me and I wasn't sure, when I unlocked the door to the brownstone we live in and went up to our third-floor apartment, if I even wanted to see Mom before I'd had time to think. My mother's a very good person to talk to; most of the time she can help us sort out problems, even when we're wrong, without making us feel like worms. But as it turned out, I didn't have to worry about whether I was going to be able to think things through before I talked to her this time, because she wasn't home. She'd left a note for us on the kitchen table:

L and C—
At neighborhood association
meeting. New cookies in jar.
Help yourselves.
Love, Mom

Mom always—well, usually—baked cookies for us when she knew she wasn't going to be home. Chad says she still does; it's as if she feels guilty for not being a 100 percent housewife, which of course no one but she herself expects her to be.

After I'd skimmed a few cookies off the top of the pile in the jar, and was sitting there at the table eating them and wishing the baseball season lasted into November so there'd be a game on to take my mind off school, I saw the second note under the first one:

31

Liza—
Someone named Annie something
—Cannon? Kaynon?—called. She
said would you please call her, 877-
9384. Have another cookie.
Love, Mom

I didn't know why, but as soon as I saw that note, I felt my heart starting to beat faster. I also realized I was now thoroughly glad Mom wasn't home, because I didn't want anyone around when I called Annie, though again I didn't know why. My mouth felt dry, so I got a drink of water, and I almost dropped the glass because my hands were suddenly sweaty. Then I went to the phone and started dialing, but I stopped in the middle because I didn't know what I was going to say. I couldn't start dialing again till I told myself a few times that since Annie had called me, thinking of what to say was up to her.

Someone else answered the phone—her mother, I found out later—and I found myself feeling jealous of whoever it was for being with Annie while I was all the way down in Brooklyn Heights, not even on the same island she was.

Finally Annie came to the phone and said, "Hello?"

"Annie." I think I managed to sound casual, at least I know I tried to. "Hi. It's Liza."

"Yes," she said, sounding really happy. "I recognized your voice. Hi." There was a little pause, and I could feel my heart thumping. "Hey," Annie said, "you called back!"

It struck me then that she didn't know what to say any more than I did, and for a few seconds we both just fumbled. But after about the third very long pause she said, low and hesitant, "Um—I was wondering if you'd like to go to the Cloisters with me Saturday. Don't if you don't want to. I thought maybe you'd like it since you go to the Metropolitan so much, but—oh, well, maybe you wouldn't."

"Sure I would," I said quickly.

"You would?" She sounded surprised.

"Sure. I love it up there. The park, everything."

"Well—well, maybe if it's a nice day I'll bring a picnic, and we could eat it in the park. We wouldn't even have to go into the museum."

"I like the museum. Just as much as the park." I felt myself smiling. "Just promise me you won't rearrange the statues or pose in front of a triptych or anything when someone's looking."

Annie laughed then—I think that was the first time I heard her laugh in her special way. It was full of delight— I don't mean delightful, although it was that, too. She laughed as if what I'd just said was so clever that it had somehow made her bubble over with joy.

That phone call was the best thing that had happened all day, and for a while after I'd hung up, the situation at school didn't seem nearly so bad any more.

4

Ms. Widmer was a couple of minutes late to English on Friday, which was my last class for the day. She gave us a quick nod, picked up the poetry book we'd been studying, and read:

> "Out of the night that covers me,
>   Black as the Pit from pole to pole,
> I thank whatever gods may be
>   For my unconquerable soul."

As carefully as I could, I folded up the architecture review Dad had clipped for me from his *New York Times*—I'd been reading it to keep my mind off the student council hearing, which was that afternoon—and listened. Mom once said that Ms. Widmer's voice was a cross between Julie Harris's and Helen Hayes's. I've never heard either of them that I know of, so all I can say is that Ms. Widmer had the kind of voice, especially when she read poetry, that made people listen.

> "In the fell clutch of circumstance
>   I have not winced nor cried aloud."

Ms. Widmer looked up, pushing her gray bangs out of her eyes. She wasn't old, but she was prematurely gray. Sometimes she joked about it, in the special way she had of finding humor in things most people didn't find funny. "What does 'fell' mean? Anyone?"

"Tripped," said Walt, with great solemnity. "He fell as he got into the bus—he had a fell—a fell fall. A fell clutch would be when he grabbed for the handle as he fell."

Ms. Widmer laughed good-naturedly along with the boos and groans and then called on Jody Crane, who was senior representative to student council. "In Tolkien," Jody said—he was very solemn and analytical—"it's used to describe people like Sauron and the Orcs and guys like that, so I guess it means evil."

"Close, Jody, close," Ms. Widmer said. She opened the leather-bound dictionary she kept on her desk and used at least three times every class period. She'd had it re-bound, she told us once, because it contained almost the entire English language and that was well worth doing something special for. "Fell," she read. "Adjective, Middle English, Anglo-Saxon, and Old French. Also Late Latin. Fierce, cruel. Poetic—" She looked up and an involuntary shudder went through the class as she lowered her voice and said the single word: "deadly." Then she turned back to the book.

"In the fell clutch of circumstance
I have not winced nor cried aloud.
Under the bludgeonings of chance
My head is bloody, but unbowed.

"Beyond this place of wrath and tears
    Looms but the horror of the shade,
And yet the menace of the years
    Finds, and shall find me, unafraid.
"It matters not how strait the gate,
    How charged with punishments the scroll,
I am the master of my fate: . . ."

Ms. Widmer paused and glanced my way for a fraction of a second before she read the last line:

"I am the captain of my soul."

"By William Ernest Henley," she said, closing the book. "1849 to 1903. British. He lost one foot to tuberculosis—TB is not always a lung disease—and nearly lost the other as well. He spent an entire year of his life in a hospital, and that led to this poem, which is called 'Invictus,' as well as to others. For homework, please discover the meaning of the word he chose for his title, and also please find and bring to class one other poem, not by Henley, but with the same theme. Due Monday."

There was a resigned groan, although no one really minded. By that time, Ms. Widmer's love of poetry had spread to most of us as if it were some kind of benign disease. It was rumored that before graduation every year she gave each senior a poem that she thought would be personally appropriate for his or her future.

For most of the rest of the period, we discussed why being in a hospital might lead to writing poems, and what kinds of poems it might lead to, and Ms. Widmer read us some other hospital poems, some of them funny, some of them sad. When the bell rang, she'd just finished a funny one. "Good timing," she said, smiling at us as the laughter died away. Then she said, "Have a good weekend," and left.

"Coming?" asked Jody, passing my desk on his way out.

"You go ahead, Jody," I said, still thinking of "Invictus" and half wondering if Ms. Widmer had really read it for me, the way it had seemed. "I think I'll see if I can find Sally." I smiled, trying to make light of it. "Criminals should stick together."

Jody smiled back and put his hand on my arm for a second. "Good luck, Liza."

"Thanks," I said. "I guess I'm going to need it."

I met Sally standing outside the Parlor, the room where council meetings were held, talking with Ms. Stevenson. Ms. Stevenson looked a little paler than usual, and her eyes already had the determined look they often had when she was doing her job as faculty adviser to student council. But otherwise she acted as if she were trying to be reassuring.

"Hi," she said cheerfully when I came up to them. "Nervous?"

"Oh, no," I said. "My stomach always feels as if there's a dog chasing its tail in it."

Ms. Stevenson chuckled. "You'll be okay," she said. "Just think before you speak, both of you. Take all the time you need before you answer questions."

"Oh, God," Sally moaned. "I think I'm going to be sick."

"No, you're not," Ms. Stevenson said firmly. "Go get a drink of water. Take a deep breath. You'll be fine." She stepped aside to let Georgie Connel—Conn—the junior representative, go in. Conn winked at me from behind his thick glasses as he opened the door. He was short, with a homely face covered with pimples, but he was one of the nicest kids in the school. He had what teachers called a creative mind, and he was also very fair, maybe the fairest person on council, except of course Ms. Stevenson.

"Well," said Ms. Stevenson briskly when Sally came back from the water fountain, "I guess it's time." She smiled at both of us as if she were wishing us luck but didn't think it would be quite proper to do it out loud. And then we all went in, Ms. Stevenson first, with Sally and me following slowly.

The Parlor, like Mrs. Poindexter's office, was so dark it was funereal. It used to be a real living room—a huge one —back when the school was a mansion, but now it was more of a semi-public lounge, reserved mostly for high-level occasions like trustees' meetings and mothers' teas, but also for council meetings. The Parlor had three long sofas along the walls, and big wing chairs, and a fireplace that took up most of the wall that didn't have a sofa against it. Over the mantle hung a picture of Letitia Foster, the school's founder. I can't imagine why Letitia Foster ever founded a school; she always looked to me as if she hated kids. She looked that way that afternoon especially, as Sally and I sidled in under her frozen hostile stare like a couple of derelict crabs.

Mrs. Poindexter was already enthroned in her special dark-maroon wing chair by the fireplace, thumbing through notes on a yellow pad and looking severe behind her rimless spectacles. Everyone else was sitting around a long, highly polished table. The vice president, Angela Cariatid, who was tall and usually reminded me in more than name of those graceful, self-possessed Greek statues that hold up buildings, didn't look at all that way as we walked in. She was sitting tensely at the end of the table nearest Mrs. Poindexter's chair, clutching the gavel as if she were drowning and it was the only other thing afloat. She'd already told me she felt rotten about having to preside, which I thought was pretty nice of her.

"It's like court on TV," Sally whispered nervously as we sat down at the other end of the table.

I remember noticing how the sun came slanting through the dusty windows onto Mrs. Poindexter's gray hair—just the top of it, because of the height of the wing chair. While I was concentrating on the incongruous halo it made, Mrs. Poindexter flipped her glasses down and nodded to Angela, who rapped so hard with the gavel that it popped out of her hand and skittered across the floor.

Sally giggled.

Mrs. Poindexter cleared her throat and Angela blushed.

Conn got up and retrieved the gavel, handing it to Angela with a grave nod. "Madame Chairperson," he murmured.

I felt myself start to laugh, especially when Sally smirked at me.

"Order!" poor Angela squeaked, and Mrs. Poindexter glared at Conn. Angela coughed and then said, pleading, "The meeting will please come to order. This—er—this is a disciplinary hearing instead of a regular meeting. Regular council business is—um—deferred till next time. Sally Jarrell and Liza Winthrop have both broken the reporting rule, and Sally Jarrell has . . ."

"Are *accused* of breaking," Ms. Stevenson interrupted quietly.

Mrs. Poindexter pinched her nose, scowling.

"Are accused of breaking the reporting rule," Angela corrected herself, "and Sally Jarrell has—er—is accused of acting in a—in a—" She looked helplessly at Mrs. Poindexter.

"In an irresponsible way, endangering the health of her fellow students," said Mrs. Poindexter, pushing herself out of the depths of her maroon chair. "Thank you, Angela. Before we begin," she said, "I would like to remind all of you that Foster is in the midst of a financial crisis of major proportions, and that any adverse publicity—any at all— could be extremely damaging to the fund-raising and student-recruitment campaigns that are our only hope of survival." She positioned herself in front of the fireplace, profile to us, looking dramatically up at Letitia. "Foster Academy was our dear founder's entire life, and it has become close to that for many of us on the faculty as well. But more important even than that is the indisputable fact that Foster has educated several generations of young men and women to the highest standards of decency and morality as well as to academic excellence. And now,"—she whirled around and faced Sally—"and now one Foster student has willfully harmed several others through a ridiculous and frivolous scheme to pierce their ears, and another student"—she faced me now—"in whom the entire student body has placed their trust, has done nothing to stop it. Sally Jarrell," Mrs. Poindexter finished sonorously, pointing at her with her glasses, "have you anything to say in your defense?"

Sally, who I could see was just about wiped out by then, shook her head. "No," she muttered, "no, except I'm sorry and I—I didn't think it could do any harm."

"You didn't think!" Mrs. Poindexter boomed. "You didn't think! This girl," she said, turning to the others at the table, "has been at Foster all her life, and she says she didn't think! Mary Lou, kindly ask Jennifer Piccolo if she will step in for a moment."

Mary Lou Dibbins, council's plump and very honest secretary-treasurer, pushed her chair back quickly and went out into the hall. Mary Lou was a math brain, but she'd told me that Mrs. Poindexter took care of council's financial records herself, and kept the little money council had locked up in her office safe. She wouldn't even let Mary Lou see the books, let alone work on them.

"Mrs. Poindexter," said Ms. Stevenson, "I really wonder if . . . Angela, is Jennifer's name on the agenda? I don't remember seeing it."

"N-no," stammered Angela.

"Jennifer volunteered at the last minute," Mrs. Poindexter said dryly. "*After* the agenda was typed."

Then Mary Lou came back with Jennifer, who had a bandage on one ear and looked absolutely terrified—not as if she'd volunteered at all.

"Jennifer," said Mrs. Poindexter, "please tell the council what your father said when he found out the doctor had to lance the infection on your ear."

"He—he said I shouldn't tell anyone outside school what had happened or it would ruin the campaign. And— and before that he said he was going to resign from being pub-pub-publicity chairman, but then my mother talked him into staying, unless—unless no one's punished. He—he said he'd always thought Foster was a—a school that produced young ladies and gentlemen, not . . ." Jennifer looked from Sally to me, apologizing with her frightened, tear-filled eyes, "not hoodlums."

"Thank you, Jennifer," Mrs. Poindexter said, looking pleased under her indignant surface. "You may go."

"Just a minute," said Ms. Stevenson, her voice tight, as if she were trying to hold on to her temper. "Angela, may I ask Jennifer a question?"

Angela looked at Mrs. Poindexter, who shrugged as if she thought whatever it was couldn't possibly be important.

"Angela?" said Ms. Stevenson pointedly.

"I—I guess so," said Angela.

"Jenny," Ms. Stevenson asked, gently now, "did Sally ask you to have your ears pierced?"

"No—no."

"Then why did you decide to have her pierce them?"

"Well," said Jennifer, "I saw the sign and I'd been thinking about going to Tuscan's, you know, that department store downtown, to have it done, but they charge eight dollars for only two holes, and I didn't have that much and the sign said Sally would do four holes for only six dollars—you know, one-fifty a hole—and I had that much. So I decided to go to her."

"But Sally never came to you and suggested it?"

"N-no."

"Thank you, Jenny," said Ms. Stevenson. "I hope the infection heals soon."

There was absolute silence as Jennifer walked out.

Angela looked at the piece of paper—the agenda, I suppose—in front of her and said, "Well . . ."

But Sally jumped to her feet. "Mrs. Poindexter," she said. "I—I'm sorry. I'll—I'll pay Jennifer's doctor bills. I'll pay everyone's if I can afford it. And—and I'll donate the money I made to the campaign. But I really did try to be careful. My sister had her ears done that way and she was fine, honest . . ."

"Sally," said Ms. Stevenson, again very gently, "you took bio. You know your way couldn't have been as safe as the sterile punches they use down at Tuscan's."

"I—I know. I'm sorry." Sally was almost in tears.

"Well," began Ms. Stevenson, "I think . . ."

"That will be all, then, Sally," said Mrs. Poindexter, interrupting. "We will take note of your apology. You may wait outside if you like."

"Mrs. Poindexter," Jody said, as if it had taken him all this time to work up to it, "is this really the way a disciplinary hearing's supposed to go? I mean, isn't Angela—I mean, isn't she supposed to be doing Liza's job, sort of, and running the hearing?"

"Of course," said Mrs. Poindexter, smooth as an oil slick, shrugging as if asking what she could do if Angela wouldn't cooperate. Then she turned to me. "Eliza," she said, "now that you have had a chance to think over our talk, have you anything to say? An explanation, perhaps, of why you didn't see to it that Sally was reported immediately?" She put her glasses on and looked down at her notes.

I didn't know what to say, and I wasn't sure anyway how I was going to make my tongue move in a mouth that suddenly felt as dryly sticky as the inside of a box of old raisins.

"I don't see what rule Sally broke," I said at last, slowly. "If I'd really thought she was breaking a rule, I'd have asked her to report herself, but . . ."

"The point," said Mrs. Poindexter, not even bothering to flip her glasses down, but peering at me over their tops, "as I told you in my office, has to do with the spirit of the rules—the spirit, Eliza, not a specific rule. I am sure you are aware that harming others is not the Foster way—yet you did not report Sally or ask her to report herself. And furthermore, I suspect that you did not do so because, despite being student council president, you do not believe in some of the rules of this school."

"Out of the night that covers me," suddenly echoed in my mind from English class. *"Black as the Pit . . ."*

I licked my dry lips. "That's right," I said. "I—I don't believe in the reporting rule because I think that by the time people are in Upper School they're—old enough to take responsibility for their own actions."

I could see Ms. Stevenson smiling faintly as if she approved, but she also looked worried. She raised her hand, and Angela, after glancing at Mrs. Poindexter, nodded at her.

"Liza," asked Ms. Stevenson, "suppose you saw a parent beating a child. Would you do anything?"

"Sure," I said. It suddenly became very clear, as if Ms. Stevenson had taken one of the big spotlights from up on the stage and turned it onto a place in my mind I hadn't seen clearly before. "Of course I would. I'd tell the parent to stop and if that didn't work, I'd go to the police or some-

44

one like that. I just don't think what Sally did is on the same scale."

"Even though," said Mrs. Poindexter, her voice sounding as if it were coming through gravel again, "Sally caused a number of infections and in particular infected the daughter of our publicity man?"

I got angry then. "It doesn't make any difference who got infected," I shouted. "Jennifer's no better than anyone else just because we need Mr. Piccolo." I tried to lower my voice. "The infections were bad, sure. But Sally didn't set out to cause them. In fact, she did everything she could to prevent them. And she didn't force anyone to have their ears pierced. Sure, it was a dumb thing to do in the first place. But it wasn't—oh, I don't know, some kind of—of criminal thing, for God's sake!"

Ms. Stevenson nodded, but Mrs. Poindexter's mouth pulled into a tense straight line and she said, "Anything else, Eliza?"

Yes, I wanted to say to her, *let Angela run the meeting; let me run meetings when I'm holding the gavel*—for she'd done nearly the same thing to me, many times—*student council's for the students, not for you, you old . . .*

But I managed to keep my anger back, and all I said was "No," and walked out, wanting suddenly to call Annie, even though I didn't know her very well yet and I was going to see her the next day at the Cloisters anyway.

Sally was sitting on the old-fashioned wooden settle in the hall outside the Parlor, hunched over and crying on Ms. Baxter's skinny chest. Ms. Baxter was dabbing at Sally's eyes with one of the lacy handkerchiefs she always carried in her sleeve, and chirping, "There, there, Sally, the Lord will forgive you, you know. Why, my dear child, He must see already that you are truly sorry."

"But it's so terrible, Ms. Baxter," Sally moaned. "Jennifer's ears—oh, Jennifer's poor, poor ears!"

I had never seen Sally like this.

"Hey, Sal," I said as cheerfully as I could, sitting down on the other side of her and touching her arm. "It's not terminal, she's going to get better. You did try to be careful, after all. Come on, it'll be okay. Jennifer'll be fine."

But Sally just burrowed deeper into Ms. Baxter's front.

Ms. Stevenson came out of the Parlor and beckoned to us to follow her back in. She looked kind of grim, as if she were having trouble with her temper again. I'd heard on television that when a jury takes a long time it's a good sign for the person on trial, but when they make up their minds quickly it's usually bad, and my mouth got raisiny again.

Mrs. Poindexter nodded to Angela when we came in, after looking at Ms. Stevenson as if trying to tell her that she was letting Angela run the meeting after all. Ms. Stevenson, if she noticed, didn't react.

"Um," said Angela, looking down at her paper again. "Um—Sally—Liza—the council has decided to suspend you both for one week."

"That's only three days," Mary Lou put in, "because of Thanksgiving."

"I did not," said Mrs. Poindexter, "see you raise your hand, Mary Lou. Continue, Angela."

"Um—the suspensions will be removed from your records at the end of the year if—if you don't do anything

46

else. So colleges won't know about it unless you break another rule."

"And?" prompted Mrs. Poindexter severely.

"Oh," said Angela. "Do I—do I say that, too, with Sally here and everything?"

"Sally," said Mrs. Poindexter, "is still a member of the student body."

"Well," said Angela, looking at me in a way that made my heart speed up as if I were at the dentist's. "Liza, Mrs. Poindexter said that because you're council president and —and . . ."

"And because no council president in the history of this school has ever broken the honor code—go on, Angela," Mrs. Poindexter said.

"There's—going to be a vote of confidence on the Monday after Thanksgiving to see if the kids still want you to —to be council president. But," she added hastily, "the fact that there was a vote of confidence won't go on your record unless you don't get reelected."

"Meeting adjourned," said Mrs. Poindexter, picking up her papers and leading the others out. Sally gave me a weak smile as she passed my chair.

Conn hung back for a minute. "The key," he said to me in a low voice, bending down to where I was still sitting, "was when Angie said, 'Mrs. Poindexter said'—not, 'Council said'—about the vote of confidence. I hope you caught that, Liza, because it was her idea and she's the only one for it. Ms. Stevenson got her to say the part about things not going on records. We all thought you should stay in office, and I bet the rest of the kids will, too. Heck, none of us would've turned Sally in either, not for that. A couple of kids said they might have tried harder to stop her, that was all, but I bet they wouldn't even have done that. Liza, Poindexter's so worried about the stupid fund-raising campaign, she can't even think straight." Conn reached down and squeezed my shoulder. "Liza—I'm sure you'll win."

"Thanks, Conn," I managed to say. My voice was too shaky for me to say anything else. But all I could think was, *What if I don't win and it does go on my record?*

For the first time in my life I began wondering if I really was going to get into MIT after all. And what it would do to my father, who's an engineer and had taught there, if I didn't. And what it would do to me.

5

J told my parents about the suspension Friday night while they were in the living room having a drink before dinner, which is always a good time to tell them difficult things. My father was furious. "You're an intelligent person," he thundered. "You should have shown better judgment."

My mother was sympathetic, which was worse. "She's also an adolescent," she told my father angrily. "She can't be expected to be perfect. And the school's coming down a lot harder on her than on Sally. That's not fair." My mother's a quiet person, except when she thinks something's unjust, or when she's defending me or Chad. Or Dad, for that matter. Dad's terrific, and I love him a lot, but he does expect people to be perfect, especially us, and especially me, his fellow "intelligent person."

"It's fair, all right," Dad said into his martini. "Liza was in a position of responsibility, just as Mrs. Poindexter said. She should have known better. I wouldn't expect that little twit Sally Jarrell to know how to think, let alone how to behave, but Liza . . ."

That's when I got up and left the room.

Chad thought the whole thing was funny. He came out to the kitchen, where I'd gone, on the pretext of getting a

49

Coke, and found me leaning against the refrigerator, fuming. "Pretty cool, Lize," he said, flapping one of his earlobes and wearing his isn't-life-ridiculous look.

"Oh, shove it."

"Think she'd do my ears? One gold hoop, like a pirate?"

"She'll do your nose if you don't shut up," I snapped.

"Hey, come off it." He pushed me aside and reached into the refrigerator for his Coke. "I'd give anything to be suspended." He popped the ring into the can and took a long swallow. "What are you going to do next week, anyway? Three free days and then Thanksgiving vacation—wow!" He shook his head and then brushed the hair out of his eyes. "They going to make you study?"

I hadn't thought of that and realized I'd better call school on Monday to find out. "I'll probably run away to sea," I told Chad. Then, thinking of the Cloisters and Annie, I added, "Or at least go to a lot of museums."

School seemed very far away the next day at the Cloisters with Annie, even though at first we were the way we'd been on the phone—not exactly tongue-tied, but not knowing what to say, either.

The Cloisters, which is a museum of medieval art and architecture, is in Fort Tryon Park, so far uptown it's almost out of the city. It overlooks the Hudson River like a medieval fortress, even though it's supposed to look like a monastery and does, once you get inside.

I was early so I decided to walk from the subway instead of taking the bus that goes partway into the park, but even so, Annie was there before me. As I walked up, I saw her near the entrance, leaning against the building's reddish-brown granite and looking off in the opposite direction. She had on a long cotton skirt and a heavy red sweater; I remember thinking the sweater made the skirt look out of place, as did the small backpack strapped to her shoulders. Her hair tumbled freely down over the pack.

I stopped for a few seconds and just stood there watching her, but she didn't notice me. So I went up to her and said, "Hi."

She gave a little jump, as if she'd been miles or years away in her thoughts. Then a wonderful slow smile spread across her face and into her eyes, and I knew she was back again. "Hi," she said. "You came."

"Of course I came," I said indignantly. "Why wouldn't I have?"

Annie shrugged. "I don't know. I wondered if I would. We're probably not going to be able to think of a thing to say to each other."

A bus pulled up and hordes of students with sketchbooks, plus mothers and fathers with reluctant children, had to go around us to get to the door. "All week," Annie said, watching them, "I kept, um, remembering that guard and the two little boys, didn't you?"

I had to say that I hadn't, so I told her about the ear-piercing incident to explain why.

"Because of *ear* piercing?" she said incredulously when I'd finished telling her the story. "All that fuss?"

I nodded, moving aside to let some more people through. "I guess maybe it is a little harsh," I said, trying to explain about the fund-raising campaign, "but . . ."

"A little harsh!" Annie almost shouted. "A little!" She shook her head and I guess she realized we were both getting loud, because she looked around and laughed, so I laughed, too, and then we both had to step back to let a huge family pass. The last kid was a stuck-up-looking boy of about nine with a fancy camera that had hundreds of dials and numbers. He looked more like a small robot than a kid, even when he whirled around and pointed his camera at Annie. Annie held out her big skirt like a medieval damsel and dipped into a graceful curtsy; the kid snapped her picture without even smiling. Then, when Annie straightened up into a religious-looking pose that I've seen in a hundred medieval paintings, he became a real kid for a second—he stuck his tongue out at her and ran inside.

"You're welcome," Annie called after him, sticking out her tongue, too. "The public," she sighed dramatically, "is so ungrateful. I do wish Father wouldn't insist that I pose for their silly portraits." She stamped her foot delicately, the way the medieval damsel she was obviously playing might have. "Oh, I'm so angry I could—I could spear a Saracen!"

Once again I found myself catching her mood, but more quickly this time. I bowed as sweepingly as I could and said, "Madame, I shall spear you a hundred Saracens if you bid me, and if you give me leave to wear your favor."

Annie smiled, out of character for a second, as if thanking me for responding. Then she went back into her role and said, "Shall we walk in the garden, sir knight, among the herbs and away from these rude throngs, till my duties force me to return?"

I bowed again. It was funny, I wasn't nearly so self-conscious this time, even though there were crowds of

52

people around. Still being the knight, I offered Annie my arm and we strolled inside, which is the only way to get to the museum's lower level and leads to the herb garden. We paid our "donation" and went downstairs and outside again, where we sat on a stone bench in the garden and looked out over the Hudson River.

"It just seems ridiculous, Liza," Annie said after a few minutes, "to make such a fuss about anything so silly."

I knew immediately she meant the ear-piercing business again.

"In my school," she went on, sliding her backpack off and turning to me, "kids get busted all the time for assault and possession and things like that. There are so many security people around, you have to remind yourself it's school you're in, not jail. But at your school they get upset about a couple of infected ears! I can't decide if it's wonderful that they don't have anything more serious to worry about—or terrible." Annie grinned and flipped back some of her hair, showing me a tiny pearl earring in each ear. "I did mine myself," she said. "Two years ago. No infection."

"Maybe you were lucky," I said, a little annoyed. "I wouldn't let Sally pierce mine."

"That's just you, though. I can't imagine you with pierced ears, anyway." She buried her face in a lavender bush that was growing in a big stone pot next to the bench. "If you ever want it done," she said into the bush, "I'll do it for you. Free."

I had an absurd desire to say, "Sure, any time," but that was ridiculous. I knew I didn't have the slightest wish to have my ears pierced. In fact, I'd always thought the whole custom barbaric.

Annie broke off a sprig of lavender and I could see from the way she pushed her small shoulders back and sat up straighter that she was the medieval damsel again. "My favor, sir knight," she said gravely, handing me the lavender. "And will you wear it into battle?"

"Madame," I said, getting up quickly so I could bow again. "I will wear it even unto death." Then my self-consciousness returned and I felt my face getting red, so I held the lavender up to my nose and sniffed it.

"Good sir," said Annie, "surely so gallant and skilled a knight as you would never fall in battle."

I'm not this clever, I wanted to say, panicking; *I can't keep up with you—please stop.* But Annie was looking at me expectantly, so I went on—quickly, because the huge family with the obnoxious shutterbug was about to come through the door that led out to the garden. "Madame," I said, trying to remember my King Arthur but sounding more like Shakespeare than like Malory, "when I carry your favor, I carry your memory. Your memory brings your image to my mind, and your image will ever come between me and my opponent, allowing him to unhorse me with one thrust."

Annie extended her hand, palm up, for the lavender.

"Hold it!" ordered the robot kid, peering at us through his viewfinder.

"Then return my favor quickly, sir knight," said Annie, not moving, "for I would not have you fall."

I handed the lavender back to her, and the kid's professional-sounding shutter clicked and whirred.

It was as if the sound of the camera snapped us back into the real world, because even though the kid and his family were obviously not going to stay in the garden long, Annie picked up her pack and said matter-of-factly, "Are you hungry for lunch? Or should we go in and look around? The sad virgin," she said, looking dolefully down at the ground, imitating one of my favorite statues; "the angry lion?" She made a twirling motion above her mouth and I knew right away she was impersonating the wonderful lion fresco in the Romanesque Hall; he has a human-looking mustache. "Or"—she stood up and glanced nervously around the garden, one wrist bent into a graceful, cautious hoof—"or the unicorns?"

"Unicorns," I said, amazed at the speed with which she could go from one character to another and still capture the essence of each.

"Good," she said, dropping her hand. "I like them best." She smiled.

I got up, saying, "Me, too," and we stood there facing each other for a moment, not saying anything more. Then Annie, as if she'd read my thoughts, said softly, "I don't know if I believe any of this is happening or not."

But before I could answer she gave me a little push and said, in a totally different voice, "Come on! To the unicorns!"

The unicorn tapestries are in a quiet room by themselves. There are seven, all intact except one, which is only a fragment. All of them, even though they're centuries old, are so bright it's hard to believe that the colors must have faded over the years. Together they tell the story of a unicorn hunt, complete with lords, ladies, dogs, long spears, and lots of foliage and flowers. Unfortunately, the hunters wound the unicorn badly—in one tapestry he looks dead

—but the last one shows him alive, wearing a collar and enclosed in a circular pen with flowers all around. Most people seem to notice the flowers more than anything else, but the unicorn looks so disillusioned, so lonely and caged, that I hardly see the flowers at all—but the unicorn's expression always makes me shiver.

I could tell from Annie's face as she stood silently in front of the last tapestry that she felt exactly the same way, even though neither of us spoke. Then a woman's voice shrilled, "Caroline, how often do I have to tell you *not* to touch?"—and in came a big crowd of people along with a flat-voiced tour guide: "Most of the unicorn tapestries were made as a wedding present for Anne of Britanny."

Annie and I left quickly.

We went outside and walked in silence away from the Cloisters and well into Fort Tryon Park, which is so huge and wild it can almost make you forget you're in the city. There'd been more rain during the week and it had washed the last of the leaves off the trees. Now the leaves were lying soggily underfoot, but some of them were still bright in the chilly fall sunshine.

Annie found a large flat rock, nearly dry, and we sat on it. Her pack got stuck when she hunched her shoulders to take it off, and when I helped her get it free, I could feel how thin her shoulders were, even under the heavy sweater.

"Egg salad," she said in an ordinary voice, unwrapping foil packages. "Cheese and ketchup. Bananas, spice cake." She smiled. "I can't vouch for the cake because it's the first one I've ever made, and my grandmother had to keep giving me directions. There's coffee, too. You'd probably rather have wine, but I didn't have enough money, and they don't always believe I'm eighteen."

"Are you?"

Annie shook her head. "Seventeen," she said, and I said, "Coffee's fine, anyway." Oddly enough, it had never occurred to me to have wine at a picnic, but as soon as Annie mentioned it, it sounded terrific.

Annie carefully unwrapped two big pieces of cake and put them on neat squares of foil. Then, with no transition at all, she said, "Actually, sir knight, this plate is from my father's castle. I had my maid take it this morning for this very use. The sliced boar," she said, handing me an egg salad sandwich, "is, I'm afraid, indifferent, but the peacocks' tongues"—this was a banana—"are rather nice this year."

"Best boar I've ever had," I said gallantly, taking a bite of my sandwich. It wasn't bad as egg salad, either.

Annie spread her skirt neatly around her and ate a cheese-and-ketchup sandwich while I finished my egg one; we were quiet again.

"The mead," I said, to make conversation after I'd taken a sip of coffee, "is excellent."

Annie held up a couple of packs of sugar and a small plastic bag of Cremora. "Do you really take your mead black? I brought this in case."

"Always," I said solemnly. "I have always taken my mead black."

Annie smiled and picked up her cake. "You must think I'm an awful child," she said with her mouth full. "I forget most people don't like pretending that way after they're much older than seven."

57

"Did I look," I asked her, "as if I didn't like it?"

She smiled, shaking her head, and I told her about how I'd acted out King Arthur stories up until I was fourteen, and how I still sometimes thought about them. That led to both of us talking about our childhoods and our families. She told me she had a married sister in Texas she hadn't seen for years, and then she told me about her father, who was born in Italy and is a cab driver, and her grandmother, who lives with them and who was born in Italy, too. Annie's last name hadn't started out as Kenyon at all, but something very long and complicated in Italian which her father had Anglicized.

"What about your mother?" I asked.

"She was born here," Annie said, finishing her cake while I ate my banana. "She's a bookkeeper—supposedly part-time, but she stays late a lot. The other day she said she's thinking of working full-time next year, when I'm in college. Assuming Nana—my grandmother—is still mostly well, and assuming I get into college in the first place." She laughed. "If I don't, maybe I'll be a bookkeeper, too."

"Do you think you won't get in?" I asked.

Annie shrugged. "I probably will. My marks are okay, especially in music. And my SAT scores were good."

Then we talked about SAT's and marks for a while. Most of that afternoon was—how can I put it? It felt a little as if we'd found a script that had been written just for us, and we were reading through the beginning quickly —the imaginative, exploratory part back in the museum, and now the factual exposition: "What's your family like? What's your favorite subject?"—hurrying so we could get to the part that mattered, whatever that was to be.

Annie put out her hand for my banana skin. "My first choice," she was saying—the factual part of the script still —"is Berkeley."

"Berkeley?" I said, startled. "In California?"

She nodded. "I was born there—well, in San José, which isn't that far from Berkeley. Then we moved to San Francisco. I love California. New York's—unfriendly." She stuffed the empty skin into her pack. "Except for you. You're the first really friendly person I've met since high school—the whole time we've lived here."

"Oh, come on," I said, flattered. "That can't be true."

She smiled, stretching. "No? Come to my school next week while you're suspended. You'll see." She sat there quietly, still smiling at me, then shook her head and looked down at the rock, poking at a bit of lichen. "Weird," she said softly.

"What is?"

She laughed, not a full-of-delight laugh this time, but a short, troubled one. "I almost said something—oh, something crazy, that's all. I guess I don't understand. Not quite, anyway." She shouldered her pack and stood up before I could ask her to explain. "It's getting late," she said. "I've got to go. Are you walking to the subway? Or taking the bus?"

The next day—Sunday—started out horribly. It was drizzling out, so we all sat stiffly around the apartment with the *Times*, trying not to talk about suspension or earrings or anything related. But that didn't last long. "Look, George," Mom said from her corner of the sofa as soon as she opened the paper. "The cutest pair of gold earrings—

do you think Annalise would like them?" Annalise is her sister and had a birthday coming up.

Dad glared at me and said, "Ask Liza. She knows more about earrings than anyone else in the family."

Then Dad found an article about discipline problems in high schools, which he insisted on reading aloud, and Chad, who was sprawled out on the floor at the foot of Dad's big yellow chair, found a court case involving a kid who'd broken into his school's office safe in revenge for being expelled.

When I couldn't stand it any more I got up from my end of the sofa and went out for a walk on the Promenade, which is also called the Esplanade. It's a wide, elevated walkway that runs along one side of Brooklyn Heights, above New York Harbor and the beginning of the East River. It's nice; you can see the Manhattan skyline, and the Statue of Liberty, and the Staten Island ferry chugging back and forth, and of course the Brooklyn Bridge, which links Brooklyn to Manhattan and is just a few blocks away. Only that day the weather was so dismal I couldn't see much of anything except my own bad mood. I was leaning against the cold wet railing, staring out at a docked freighter, but really going back and forth with myself over whether I should have tried harder to stop Sally, when a voice at my elbow said, "Don't jump"—and there was Annie. She was wearing jeans again, and some kind of scarf, and her cape.

"But," I stammered, "but—but how . . ."

She pulled out the notebook from when we'd exchanged addresses and waved it at me. "I wanted to see where you live," she said, "and then there I was at your building so

I rang the bell, and then your mother—she's pretty—said you'd gone for a walk, and then this kid—your brother, Chad, I guess—came out after me and said he thought this was where you'd probably be and told me how to get here. He seems nice."

"He—he is." It wasn't much to say, but I was still so bewildered and so happy at the same time that I couldn't think of anything else.

"Nice view," said Annie, leaning against the railing next to me. Then in a very quiet, serious voice she said, "What's the matter, Liza? The suspension?"

It was as if the script that had been written for us had suddenly jumped way ahead.

"Yes," I said.

"Walk with me," Annie said, stuffing her hands into her jeans pockets under her cape.

"My Nana says," Annie told me, "that walking helps the mind work. She used to hike out into the countryside from her village in Sicily when she was a girl. She used to climb mountains, too." Annie stopped and looked at me. "She told me once, back when we were in California, that the thing about mountains is that you have to keep on climbing them, and that it's always hard, but that there's a view from the top, every time, when you finally get there."

"I don't see how that . . ." I began.

"I know. You're student council president, but you're really just a person. Probably a pretty good one, but still just a person. Because you're student council president, everyone expects you to be perfect, and that's hard. Try-ing to live up to everyone's expectations and being yourself, too—maybe that's a mountain you have to go on climbing. Nana would say"—Annie turned, making me stop—"that it'll be worth it when you get to the top. And I'd say go on climbing, but don't expect to reach the top tomorrow. Don't expect yourself to be perfect for other people."

"For a unicorn," I think I said, "you're pretty smart."

Annie shook her head. We talked about it a little more, and then we went on walking along the dreary, wet Promenade, talking about responsibility and authority and even about God—no pretending this time, no medieval improvisations, just us. By the time we were through, I realized I was talking to Annie as if I'd known her all my life, not just a few days. Annie? I'm not sure how she felt. She still hadn't said much about herself, personal things, I mean, and I had.

By about four o'clock we were so cold and wet that we went up to Montague Street, which is the main shopping street for the Heights, and had a cup of coffee. We started getting silly again—reading the backs of sugar packages aloud and imitating other customers and laughing. When Annie blew a straw paper at me, the waitress glared at us, so we left.

"Well," said Annie, on the sidewalk outside the coffee shop.

"Their mead," I said, reluctant for her to leave, "wasn't half as good as yours."

"No," said Annie. "Liza . . . ?"

"What?"

Then we both spoke at once.

"You first," I said.

62

"No, you."

"Well, I was just going to say that if you don't have to go yet, you could come back to my apartment and see my room or something. But it's almost six . . ."

"And *I* was going to say that if you don't have to eat supper right away, maybe I could come back to your apartment and see your room."

"Supper," I said, looking up to see what color the traffic light was, and then crossing the street with Annie, "is sometimes pretty informal on Sundays. Maybe Mom will even invite you . . ."

Mom did, and Annie phoned her mother, who said she could stay. We had baked ham and scalloped potatoes, so it wasn't one of our informal and easily expandable Sunday suppers, which usually was eggs in some form, cooked by Dad. But there was plenty of food, and everyone seemed to like Annie. In fact, as soon as Mom found out Annie was a singer, they began talking about Bach and Brahms and Schubert so much that I felt left out and revived a friendly running argument I had with Dad about the Mets versus the Yankees. Mom got the point in a few minutes and changed the subject.

Toward dessert, I started panicking about my room, which was a mess—so much so, I suddenly remembered, that I almost didn't want to show it to Annie after all. It's a fairly large room, with a lot of pictures of buildings fastened to the walls with drawing tape, and as soon as we went inside I saw how shabby some of the drawings had gotten and how dirty the tape was. But Annie didn't seem to mind.

She went right to my drawing table—that was actually

the best thing about my room anyway—on which was a pretty good preliminary sketch for my solar-house project. Right away she asked, "What's this?" so I started explaining, and showed her some of the other sketches I'd done. Although most people get bored after about five minutes of someone's explaining architectural drawings, Annie sat down on the stool by the drawing table and kept asking questions till nearly ten o'clock, when Mom came in to say she thought it was time for Dad to take Annie home. At that point I realized that Annie really seemed interested in architecture, and I felt embarrassed for starting that show-off argument at dinner instead of listening to her talk.

Dad and Chad and I all ended up taking Annie home on the subway, which turned out to be a longer trip than we'd expected. On the way I tried asking one or two questions about music, but it was too noisy for conversation. Just before we got to her stop, Annie gave my hand a quick squeeze and said, "You don't have to do that, Liza."

"Do what?"

"Talk about music with me. It's okay. I know you don't like it all that much."

"Liza," Chad called, "I can't hold this door all night. Girls!" he said disgustedly to Dad when we were finally out of the train.

"I like music fine," I said to Annie, falling behind my father and Chad as we all went up the stairs to the street. "Really. Why, I . . ." Then I stopped, because Annie was laughing, seeing through me. "Okay, okay," I said. "I don't know anything about music. But I—am—willing—to learn."

"Fine," said Annie. "You can come to my next recital. There's one before Christmas."

By this time we were up on the street, and for the few blocks to Annie's building I tried again to ask her questions, nontechnical ones, about the recital and what kinds of songs she liked to sing and things like that. She seemed to be answering carefully, as if she were trying to make me feel I understood more than I did.

"Well," said Dad when we got to Annie's building—a big ugly yellow brick oblong in the middle of almost a whole block of abandoned brownstones—"why don't we see you up to your apartment, Annie?"

"Oh, no, Mr. Winthrop," she said quickly—and I realized that she was embarrassed. "I'll be fine."

"No, no," Dad said firmly, "we'll take you up."

"Dad . . ." I said under my breath—but he ignored me, and we all rode silently up to the fifth floor in a rickety elevator that seemed to take long enough to get to the top of the Empire State Building.

Annie's front door was near the elevator, a little to the left down a dark shabby hall, and I had to admit that Dad was probably right to have us all go up there with her. But I could see she was still embarrassed, so I said, "Well, good night," as loudly and as cheerfully as possible, and practically pushed Dad and Chad back into the elevator.

Annie waved to me from her door, and her lips formed the words "Thank you" silently as the elevator door closed.

When we got back out onto the street, I felt as if I were about to burst with I didn't quite know what, so I started whistling.

"Liza," said Dad—he can be a little stiff sometimes—

"don't do that. This isn't a terrific neighborhood. Don't call attention to yourself."

"It is so a terrific neighborhood," I said, ignoring a drunk in a doorway and a skinny collarless dog who was sniffing around an overflowing litter basket. "It's a gorgeous neighborhood, beautiful, stupendous, magnificent!"

Chad tapped his head with his forefinger and said, "Crazy," to Dad. "Maybe a stop at Bellevue?" Bellevue is a huge hospital with a very active psycho ward.

I made a growling sort of werewolf noise and lunged at Chad just as a bum reeled up to Dad and asked him for seventy-five cents for the subway. So I growled at the bum, too, and he reeled away, staring at me over his shoulder.

Dad shot me a look that was supposed to be angry, but he couldn't keep it from turning into a guffaw, and then he put one arm around me and the other around Chad and marshaled us firmly over to the next block where he hailed a cab. "I can't risk being seen with you two," he grinned, giving the driver our address. "Can't you just see the *Times*? 'Prominent Engineer Seen At Large With Two Maniacs. Sanity Questioned. One Maniac A Suspended High-School Student. Ear-Piercing Ring Rumored.'"

I sneaked a surprised look at Dad and he reached over and mussed my hair in a way he hadn't done since I was little. "It's okay, Liza," he said. "We all make mistakes. That was a big one, that's all. But I know you won't do anything like it again."

But, oh, God, neither of us had any way of knowing that I would do something much, much worse—at least in the eyes of the school and my parents, and probably a whole lot of other people, too, if they'd known about it.

*L*iza took Annie's picture out of the drawer she'd been keeping it in, put it on her bureau, and went to bed.

But she couldn't sleep. She tried to read and the words blurred; she tried to draw and couldn't concentrate. Finally, she went to her desk and read through Annie's letters. "I miss you," all but the last one said at the end.

Liza took some cassettes from her bookcase—Brahms, Bach, Schubert; she put on the Schubert and went back to bed, listening.

Maybe I should stop, she thought more than once; I should probably stop thinking about this.

But although the next day she took two long walks, went to the library, and put in three unnecessary lab hours to avoid it, she was back at her desk after dinner, looking at Annie's picture and remembering . . .

6

Monday morning, just before first period, I called school and asked for Ms. Stevenson. But Ms. Baxter, who answered the phone, said she was home sick.

I thought for a minute and then, because I didn't want to talk to Mrs. Poindexter, I asked for Ms. Stevenson's home number. "This is Liza Winthrop," I said uncomfortably. "I guess you know I was suspended Friday. I, um, don't know if I'm supposed to do homework or how I'm supposed to keep up with classes or anything."

There was a pause, during which I imagined Ms. Baxter taking out one of her lace handkerchiefs and dabbing mournfully at her eyes. "Six-two-five," she said, as if she were praying, "eight-seven-one-four."

"Thank you." I clicked the receiver button and began dialing again.

Ms. Stevenson's phone rang five times, with no answer. I was just about to hang up and call Sally to see if by some chance she knew what we were supposed to do, when a voice, not Ms. Stevenson's, answered.

"Um," I said eloquently, "this—um—is Liza Winthrop, one of Ms. Stevenson's students at Foster? Well, I'm sorry to bother her if she's not feeling well, but the thing is . . ."

"Oh, Liza," the voice said. "This is Ms. Widmer. Isabelle—I mean Ms. Stevenson—has a terrible cold and I was just about to leave for school—late, as you can see. Is there anything I can do?"

I remembered then that someone had once said they thought that Ms. Stevenson and Ms. Widmer lived together.

"Or," Ms. Widmer was suggesting, "would you rather talk to her directly? It's just that she feels very rotten."

"No, it's okay," I said quickly, and explained.

Ms. Widmer left for a couple of minutes and then came back and said yes, I did have to keep up and she'd send my homework to me via Chad if that was okay and wasn't it nice it was a short week because of Thanksgiving. She suggested I get in touch with Sally to tell her it would be a good idea for her to make some kind of arrangement, too. So I called Sally—she still sounded upset about everything—and then I spent the next twenty minutes deciding what to wear to Annie's school. I must have put on four different pairs of jeans before I found one that wasn't dirty or torn or too shabby or not shabby enough, and then I darned a hole in the elbow of my favorite gray sweater, which I'd been putting off doing since spring. By the time I left, it was after ten o'clock.

It took me more than an hour to get to Annie's school, what with changing subways and all. She'd drawn me a rough floor plan of the building and copied down her schedule for me, but she'd also warned me I wouldn't be able to just walk in, as someone pretty much could at my school—and she couldn't have been more right about that! As soon as I saw the building, I remembered her comparing it to a prison. I've seen big ugly schools all over New York, but this was the worst one of all. It was about as imaginative in design as a military bunker.

I went up the huge concrete steps outside, through big double doors that had wire mesh over their windows, as did the regular windows, and into a dark cavernous hall with metal stairwells off it. The first thing that hit me was the smell: a combination of disinfectant, grass, and the subway on a hot day, with the last one of those the strongest. The second thing that hit me was how the prison atmosphere continued inside. Even the interior glass windows, on doors and looking into offices, were reinforced with wire mesh. And right in the middle of the hall, opposite the doors, was an enormous table with three security guards standing around it.

The biggest of them strode up to me the minute I walked in. "What do *you* want?" he demanded belligerently.

I told him my name, as Annie had warned me I'd have to, and said I was a friend of Annie's and had come to see the school.

"How come you're not in school yourself?" he asked.

I didn't know what to say to that. I thought of saying I was a dropout or that my school had all week off for Thanksgiving or that I'd graduated early—anything but that I'd been suspended. But then I figured I was in enough trouble already, and besides, I've always been a terrible liar, so I told the truth.

He asked why I'd been suspended, so I told him that, too.

And that did it.

He and another guard herded me into a little office off the hall. Then he asked how I'd like it if they called Foster to verify my story, and the other guard asked if I'd mind emptying my pockets, and when I said, "What for?" he looked at his cohort and said, "Is this kid for real?" Needless to say, I never did get any farther inside Annie's school that day.

So I left, and spent the next few hours at the Museum of the American Indian. When I got back, at about two-thirty, the guards and a couple of cops were outside and what seemed like thousands of kids were pouring out the doors—and just as I was thinking there was no way Annie was going to find me except by luck, I spotted her and yelled, waving my arms. One of the guards started edging toward me, but I managed to duck out of his way and get lost in the crowd; Annie watched from the next-to-top step till I crossed the street, and then she came toward me, smiling.

"Let's get away from here," she said, and led me around the corner to a quiet little park where there were mothers and baby carriages and dogs—a different world.

"I tried to get in," I said, and explained.

"Oh, Liza, I'm sorry!" she said when I was through. "I should have warned you more—I'm sorry."

"Hey, it's okay."

"Those security guards are jerks," she said, still sounding upset. "They probably thought you were selling." She gave an odd little half laugh and sat down on a bench. "We could use fewer of them here at school and more where I live."

"I didn't think it was so bad," I said, remembering her embarrassment when we took her home. "Where you live, I mean." I sat down next to her.

"Oh, come on!" said Annie, exploding the way she had at the Cloisters over the ear piercing. "You know what goes on in those buildings, the ones no one lives in? Kids shoot up, drunks finish off their bottles and then throw up all over the sidewalk, muggers jump out at you—sure, it's a wonderful neighborhood!"

"I'm sorry," I said humbly. "I guess I don't know much about it."

"That's okay," Annie said after a minute.

But it didn't seem okay to me, because there we were sitting moodily on a cold bench saying "I'm sorry" to each other for things we couldn't help. Instead of being happy to see Annie, which I'd been at first, now I felt rotten, as if I'd said something so dumb the whole friendship was going to be over with when it had only just started. *Finis* —end of script.

Annie poked her foot at a bunch of dry cracked leaves near one end of the bench; we were sitting pretty far away from each other. "Somewhere out there," she said softly, "there's someplace *right*, there's got to be." She turned to me, smiling and less upset, as if she'd forgiven me or maybe never even been as angry as she'd seemed. "Where we lived when I was little, after we'd moved to San Francisco, you could see out over the Bay—little white specks of houses nestled in the hills like—like little white birds. Getting back there and finding out if it's as beautiful as I remember—that's one of my mountains." She flapped her arms in her coat—it was thicker than her cape, but I

73

could see that it was old, even threadbare in spots. "Sometimes then I used to pretend I was a bird, too, like the ones I pretended were across the Bay, and that I could fly over to where they were."

"And now," I said carefully, "you're going to fly across the whole country to get to them."

"Oh, Liza," she said. "Yes. Yes—except . . ."

But instead of finishing she shook her head, and when I asked her "What?" she jumped up and said, "I know what let's do! Let's walk over to the IRT and go downtown and take the ferry back and forth to Staten Island till it gets dark so we can see the lights—have you ever done that? It's neat. You can pretend you're on a real ship —let's see. Where do you want to go? France? Spain? England?"

"California," I said, without thinking. "I'd like to help you find your white birds."

Annie put her head to one side, for a moment reminding me of the way she'd pretended to be a unicorn at the Cloisters. "Maybe there are white birds in Staten Island," she said softly.

"Then," I said, "I guess we should go on a quest for white birds there. California's very far away."

"That's what I was thinking before," Annie said—we were walking now, toward the subway. "But next year's far away, too."

I wondered if it really was.

On the subway, Annie's mood changed, and mine did too. After we sat down, Annie whispered, "Have you ever stared at people's noses on the subway till they don't make sense any more?" I said I hadn't, and then of course we both stared all the way to South Ferry, till people began scowling at us and moving uncomfortably away.

We rode back and forth on the Staten Island ferry for the rest of the afternoon, sometimes pretending we were going through the Panama Canal to California after all, and sometimes pretending we were going to Greece, where I was going to show Annie the Parthenon and give her architecture lessons.

"Only if I can give you history ones," she said. "Even if they hardly teach it at all at my stupid school."

"How come you know so much then?" I said, thinking of our improvisations.

"I read a lot," she said, and we both laughed.

After about four trips back and forth, the ferry crew caught on that we'd only paid once, so the next time we pulled into St. George, Staten Island, we got off and hiked up one of the hilly streets that lead away from the ferry slips, till we got to some houses with little yards in front of them. Annie said, serious again, "I'd like to live in a house with a yard someday, wouldn't you?" and I said, "Yes," and for a while we played a quiet—shy, too—game of which of the houses there we'd live in if we could. Then we sat down on a stone wall at the corner of someone's yard—it was beginning to get dark by then—and were silent for a while.

"We're in Richmond," Annie said suddenly, startling me. "We're early settlers and . . ." Then she stopped and I could feel, rather than see, that she was shaking her head. "No," she said softly. "No, I don't want to do that with you so much any more."

75

"Do what?"

"You know. Unicorns. Maidens and knights. Staring at noses, even. I don't want to pretend any more. You make me—want to be real."

I was looking for some way to answer that when a woman came out of a house across the street, carrying a mesh shopping bag and leading a little dog on a leash. When she reached the corner, she put the shopping bag into the dog's mouth and said, "Good Pixie, good girl, carry the bag for Mommy," and we both burst into helpless laughter.

When we stopped laughing, I said, awkwardly, "I'm glad you want to be real, but—well, please don't be too real. I mean . . ."

Annie gave me a funny look and said, "Annie Kenyon's dull, huh?"

"No!" I protested. "No, not dull at all. Annie Kenyon's . . ."

"What? Annie Kenyon's what?"

I wanted to say *fascinating*, because that's really what I was thinking, but I was too embarrassed. Instead, I said "Interesting," but then that sounded flat, and I knew Annie couldn't see my face clearly in the twilight anyway, so I added "Fascinating" after all. I thought *magical*, too, but I didn't say that, even though just sitting there in the growing darkness with Annie was so special and so unlike anything that had ever happened to me before that magical seemed like a good word for it and for her.

"Oh, Liza," Annie said, in a way I was beginning to expect and hope for. Then she said, "So are you," and I said stupidly, "So am I what?" Instead of answering, Annie pointed down the street to where Pixie and Mommy were coming back. Then, when I was looking at them— the streetlights were on now—Annie said very softly, "Fascinating."

Pixie was still carrying the shopping bag, but now it had a head of lettuce in it. Pixie was so low to the ground that the bag was bumping along the sidewalk.

"I hope," Annie said, "that Mommy's planning to wash that lettuce."

We sat huddled together on the wall in the shadow of some big trees, watching until Pixie and Mommy were back inside their house, and then we walked back down to the ferry slip, shoulders touching. I think one reason why we didn't move away from each other was because if we had, that would have been an acknowledgment that we were touching in the first place.

We each called home to say we'd be late, and on the way back in the ferry we stood as far up in the bow as possible so we could watch the lights in Manhattan twinkling closer and closer as we approached. We were the only people on deck; it was getting very cold.

"Look," said Annie. She closed her hand on mine and pointed up with her other hand. "The stars match the lights, Liza, look."

It was true. There were two golden lacework patterns now, one in the sky and one on shore, complementing each other.

"There's your world," Annie said softly, pointing to the Manhattan skyline, gold filigree in the distance.

"Real, but sometimes beautiful," I said, aware that I was liking Annie's hand touching mine, but not thinking beyond that.

"And that's like my world." Annie pointed up to the stars again. "Inaccessible."

"Not," I said to her softly, "to unicorns. Nothing's inaccessible to unicorns. Not even—not even white birds."

Annie smiled, as if more to herself than to me, and looked toward Manhattan again, the wind from the ferry's motion blowing her hair around her face. "And here we are," she said. "Liza and Annie, suspended in between."

We stood there in the bow for the whole rest of the trip, watching the stars and the shore lights, and it was only when the ferry began to dock in Manhattan that we moved apart and dropped each other's hands.

7

Two days later, on Wednesday, Annie managed to get out of her school long enough at lunchtime to smuggle me into the cafeteria—a huge but shabby room as crowded as Penn Station or Grand Central at Christmas. While we were sitting there trying to hear what we were saying to each other, a tall gangling kid unfolded himself from his chair, took at least a foot of heavy chain out of his pocket, and started whirling it around his head, yelling something nobody paid any attention to. In fact, no one paid any attention to the boy himself either, except for a few people who moved out of range of the swinging chain.

I couldn't believe it—I couldn't believe anyone would do that in the first place, and I also couldn't believe that if someone did, everyone would just ignore him. I guess I must have been staring, because Annie stopped in the middle of what she was saying and said, "You're wondering why that guy is swinging that chain, right?"

"Right," I said, trying to be as casual about it as she was.

"Nobody knows why he does it, but in a few minutes one of the carpentry teachers will come along and take him away—there, see?"

A large man in what I guess was a shop apron came in, ducked under the flying chain, and grabbed the kid around the waist. Right away, the kid froze, and the chain went clattering to the floor. The man picked it up, stuffed it into his pocket, and led the kid out of the cafeteria.

"Annie," I said wildly, "you mean he does that often? Why don't they take the chain away from him—I mean permanently? Why don't they . . . I don't know, you did mean he does it all the time, didn't you?"

Annie gave me a partly amused, partly sympathetic look and put down her chocolate milk carton. "He does do it all the time, once a week or so. They do take the chain away from him, but I guess he has an endless supply. I don't know why they don't do anything else about him or for him, but they don't seem to." She smiled. "You see why sometimes I prefer white birds."

"And unicorns and knights," I answered. "Good Lord!"

"When I first came here," Annie said, "I used to go home and cry at night. But after about two months of being terrified and miserable, I found out that if you keep away from everyone, they keep away from you. The only reason I never tried to transfer is because when my mother works late I go home at lunch to check on Nana. I couldn't do that if I went to another school."

"There must be *some* okay kids here," I said, looking around.

"There are. But since I spent my whole freshman year staying away from everyone, by the time I was a sophomore, everyone else already had friends." She smiled wryly, criticizing herself. "It isn't just that people in New York are unfriendly. It's also that I've been unfriendly to people in New York. Till now."

I smiled at her. "Till now," I repeated.

After lunch, since I was going to meet Annie at her apartment late that afternoon, I went to the Guggenheim Museum and tried not to think too hard about what might be happening at her school while I was safely looking at paintings. But I kept thinking about it anyway, and about how depressing a lot of Annie's life seemed to be, and about how I wished there was something I could do to make it more cheerful. The day before, after Annie got out of school, we'd gone to the New York Botanical Garden, where I'd been a couple of times with my parents, and Annie went wild walking up and down greenhouse aisles, smelling the flowers, touching them, almost talking to them. I'd never seen her so excited. "Oh, Liza," she'd said, "I never even knew this place was here—look, that's an orchid, those are impatiens, that's a bromeliad—it's like a place we used to go to in California—it's so beautiful! Oh, why can't there be more flowers in New York, more green things?"

As soon as I remembered that, standing halfway up the spiral ramp that runs through the middle of the Guggenheim, I knew what I'd do: I'd buy Annie a plant and take it to her apartment as a sort of thank-you present—thank you for what, I didn't really know, but that didn't seem to matter much as I rushed back outside to find a florist.

I found one that had some flowering plants in the window. "Do they have these in California?" I asked the man.

"Sure, sure," he said. "They have them all over."

That didn't tell me much, but I was too nervous to ask any more questions—even to ask what kind of plant the one I wanted was—it had thick furry leaves and was covered with light blue flowers. By then I knew that blue was Annie's favorite color, so I decided it probably wouldn't matter what kind of plant it was. The pot had hideous pink tinfoil wrapped around it, but I took that off in the slow elevator in Annie's building, and stuffed it into my pocket.

I remembered to knock at Annie's door—she'd told me the buzzer didn't work—and in a few minutes a quavery voice said, "Who is it?"

"Liza Winthrop," I said, and then said it again, louder, because I heard something rattling under where the peephole was.

When the door opened, I had to look down suddenly, because I'd been ready to say hello to someone at eye level. But the person who opened the door was a tiny, fragile-looking woman in a wheelchair. She had wonderful bright blue eyes and a little puckered mouth that somehow managed to look like Annie's, probably because of the smile.

"You must be Annie's frien'." The woman beamed at me, and as soon as I heard her accent I remembered that Annie's grandmother had been born in Italy. Sure enough, the woman said, "I'm her Nana—her gran'ma—come in, come in." Deftly, she maneuvered the wheelchair out of the doorway so I could step inside. "Annie, she help her mamma make the turk'," Annie's grandmother said. It was a second or two before I realized that "turk" was "turkey," but the wonderful smell that struck me as soon as I was inside told me my guess was right. "We make him the day-before"—it was one word, beautiful: *day*-before"; when she said it, it sounded like a song. "So on Thanksgiving we can have a good time. Come in, come in. Annie! Your frien', she's here. What a pretty flower—African violet, no?"

"I—I don't know," I said, bending a little closer so An-

82

nie's Nana could see the plant's flowers. "I don't know a thing about plants, but I just found out Annie likes them, so I brought her one."

I'd never have dared admit to most people—most kids, anyway—that I'd brought Annie a present, but this lovely old lady didn't seem to think there was anything odd about it. She clasped her gnarled hands together—and it was then that I knew where Annie had gotten her laugh as well as her smile, because her grandmother laughed in exactly the same way.

"Annie, she be very happy," Nana said, her bright eyes twinkling into mine, "very happy—you wait till you see her room, she loves flowers! Annie, look," she said, turning her head toward Annie, who had just come out of the kitchen, her hair braided and wrapped around her head, a dish towel around her middle, and her face red from the heat of the oven. "Look, your frien', she brought you a frien'." Nana and I chuckled at her joke as Annie looked at the violet and then at me.

"I don't believe this," Annie said, her eyes meeting mine above her grandmother's softly gleaming white hair. "You brought me an African violet?"

I nodded. "Happy Thanksgiving."

"Oh, God, Liza, I suppose you're going to tell me this is part of your real world, too, right?"

"Well," I said, feigning modesty, "it's real, all right."

"Real world, what you talk?" said Nana. "Annie, you push me in the kitchen so I can help your mamma. Then you go with your frien' and talk."

Annie winked at me as she took the back of her grandmother's chair, and Nana reached out and squeezed my hand as Annie started to wheel her past me. "I *like* you, Lize," she said, pronouncing my name the way Chad often did. "You make my Annie happy. She's so sad sometimes." Nana made the corners of her mouth droop down like a tragedy mask. "Ugh! Young girls, they should laugh. Life's bad enough when you're grown, you might as well laugh when you're young. You teach my Annie that, Lize, okay?"

"Okay," I said, looking at Annie. I think I held up my hand when I said it.

"You promise, good! Annie, she's laugh' more this week, since she met you."

Annie wheeled her grandmother into the kitchen and I stood awkwardly in the hall, looking down its dingy walls into the living room. I could see part of a very worn carpet that must once have been bright red, and a lopsided sofa with some stuffing working its way out around the edges of a couple of patches, and a faded photo of the Roman Coliseum hanging on the wall next to a cross with a dry palm leaf tucked behind it.

"Nana's," said Annie, coming back and pointing to the cross. "The rest of us aren't very religious. My mother's Protestant, and I don't know what I am." She'd taken the towel from her waist, but her face was still red and a little shiny from the heat. A wisp of her hair had begun to come loose. I wanted to push it back for her. "Nana adores you," she said.

"I adore her," I answered, as Annie led me through the living room and down a shorter but dingier hall to her room. "Listen, I take it as a solemn pledge," I said, as Annie stepped aside in the doorway so I could go into the small room, "to make you laugh, like she said. Okay?"

84

Annie smiled, but a little distantly, sat down on the edge of her narrow bed, and motioned to the only chair, which was at a table that was piled high with books and music scores and seemed to be working as a desk. "Okay," she said.

"I like your room," I told her, looking around and trying to keep away the awkwardness I was beginning to feel again. The room was tiny, but full of things that obviously meant a lot to Annie, mostly the books and music scores, but also several stuffed animals—and, as Nana had said, plants, what seemed like hundreds of them. Because of them, you didn't even notice right away that the desk-table was scarred and a bit rickety, that the bed was probably an old studio couch, and that one window had a piece of cloth stuffed in part of it, I assumed to keep out drafts. There was a big feathery fern hanging in the window and a pebble-lined tray with lots of little plants on the sill. On the floor at the foot of the bed was a plant so huge it looked like a young tree.

"Oh, come on," Annie said, "it's nothing like your room. Your room looks—shiny and, I don't know—new." Her eyes followed mine to the huge plant near the bed. "That's just a rubber tree from Woolworth's. I got it when it was little—only ninety-five cents' worth of little."

"Well, it must be a hundred dollars' worth of big now. Hey, I mean it. I like your room. I like your grandmother, I like you . . ."

For a minute, neither of us said anything. Annie looked at the floor and then went over to the rubber tree and flicked something invisible off one of its leaves. "I like you, too, Liza," she said carefully. She had put the African vio-

85

let on the desk-table, but now she picked it up and took it over to the windowsill, where she made room for it on top of the pebbles. "Humidity," she said. "They like that, and the pebbles help. I mean, the water you put in the tray for it helps—oh, damn."

She turned away from me suddenly, but something in her voice made me grab her hand and pull her around to face me again. To my astonishment, I saw that she was nearly in tears.

"What's the matter?" I asked, standing up, a little scared. "What's the matter? Did I do something?"

She shook her head, and then she rested it for a second on my shoulder. But when my hand was still on its way up to comfort her, she moved away and went to her bed-side table, where she fished a Kleenex out of a box and blew her nose. "Yes, you did something, you jerk," she said, sitting on the edge of the bed again. "You brought me a present, and I'm such a sentimental fool, it's making me cry, and I'm upset because I don't have any money to get you a present, but I wish I did."

"Oh, for God's sake," I said, and I went over and sat next to her and put my arm around her for a second. "Look, I don't want you to give me a present. That's not what this is about, is it?"

"I—I don't know," Annie said. "I never really had a friend before—that's what I was sort of trying to tell you today in the cafeteria. Well, I did in California, but I was a lot younger then, even if I did think I was going to die when she moved away—we were both in sixth grade then."

"You're the jerk," I said. "Presents aren't part of it, okay? I just knew you liked flowers, that's all, and that was exciting to me because I never knew anyone who did and I can't make anything grow to save my life. Maybe it's a thank-you present for showing me Staten Island and—and everything."

Annie sniffed loudly and finally smiled. "Okay—but that's not what this is about, either, is it? Thank-you presents—that's no good."

"Right." I got up and went back to the chair. "Tell me about your friend in California. If you want."

"Yes," said Annie. "I think I do."

For the next hour or so, I sat there in Annie's room while she showed me pictures of a pasty-faced, dull-looking little girl named Beverly and told me about how they used to go for walks on the beach and pretend they were running away, and how they used to sleep over at each other's houses, usually in the same bed, and how they giggled and talked all night and sometimes kissed each other—"the way little girls sometimes do," Annie said, reddening—I knew Annie had been pretty young then, so I didn't think anything of it. And then I asked her about her grandmother, who turned out to have made all Annie's clothes till her fingers got too stiff from arthritis. Annie said she sometimes listened to Nana breathe at night for fear she was going to die suddenly.

After a while, Annie and I went into the kitchen, where there were several cats milling around in that sideways way cats have. We sat at a round table with orange plastic place mats on it and sniffed the roasting turkey and talked to Annie's mother, who was mousy and tired-looking but nice, and to Nana, who didn't seem to me to be anywhere near dying. We drank grape juice and ate a whole plate of some wonderful Italian cookies filled with figs and dates

87

and raisins. When I left, Nana made me take a bagful of cookies home to Chad.

The next day, Thanksgiving afternoon, the doorbell rang just as I'd finished my second piece of pumpkin pie, while Dad was telling the same story he told every year, about when he and his brother swiped a Thanksgiving turkey and tried to cook it over an open fire in the woods in Maine, where he grew up. I pushed the buzzer and ran down to see who it was—and it was Annie with a short, stocky man with a black mustache, who turned out to be her father. There was a yellow cab double-parked in the street.

Annie looked as if she'd rather be on another planet.

Mr. Kenyon took off his little squashed cap and said, "We don't mean to interrupt, but Annie, she say she come down to see you this afternoon, and I say Thanksgiving is a family day and maybe you don't want company, and she say maybe I don't want her to go, so I bring her down. You gave her such a nice present—I thought maybe you and your mamma and poppa and your brother might like to come for a ride with us in the cab. That way all the families stay together and can get to know each other, too."

I looked dubiously out at the double-parked cab and then I saw Nana's cheerful face in the window, behind a fluttery wave.

"We always take my mamma for a ride in the cab on holidays," explained Mr. Kenyon.

I could tell from Annie's face that she was absolutely perishing with embarrassment, and I tried to signal her that it was okay, because it was. I could understand how she felt, but I thought her family was terrific.

88

"Let me go ask," I said, and ran upstairs.

Annie came after me and grabbed me on the first landing. "Liza, I'm sorry," she said. "He—he doesn't understand this country—I don't know, he's been here since he was twenty, but he still thinks he's back in some Sicilian village and . . ."

"I like him!" I shouted, shaking her. "I told you—I like your grandmother and the cats in your kitchen, and your mother, even though I don't know her very well, and I like your plants and your room and you, except when you're a jerk to be so worried that I'm not going to like—whatever!"

Annie smiled sheepishly and leaned against the wall. "I think it's jerky, too," she said. "I mean of me. It's just that —well, I'm always worried that people are going to laugh at them."

"Well, I'm not going to laugh at them," I said. "And if you are, I'll go live with them and you can come here and live in stuffy old Brooklyn Heights and go to Foster Academy and almost get expelled for piercing ears and—Annie?" I said, as soon as it struck me. "Are you jealous? Is that what this is really about? Do you envy me?"

"No," said Annie softly. Then she laughed a little. "No, I don't, not at all. You're right that I don't like the school I go to or the neighborhood I live in—but no, I wouldn't want to—to swap with you or anything." She smiled. "I guess you made me realize that just now, didn't you?"

"Well, good," I said, still angry, "because if you do want to swap—if that's all I mean to you, forget it."

I surprised myself, I was so mad.

89

"Oh, Liza, no," Annie said. "No. That's not what you mean to me. It's not like that at all, not at all." She edged away from the wall and then faced me, dropping a quick curtsy. "Will the Princess Eliza please to come for a ride in the magic wagon of the humble peasant? We will show her wonders—gypsies—seagulls—shining caves—the Triborough Bridge . . ."

"Oh, you nut!" I said, reaching for her hand. "You—unicorn."

For a minute we stood there looking at each other, knowing with relief that it was all right again between us.

Dad and Mom and Chad decided to stay home, though they came downstairs at my insistence to meet Mr. and Mrs. Kenyon and Nana. I think I was trying to prove to Annie that they wouldn't laugh at her family, either. Good old Chad—when he and Mom and Dad were going back in and Annie and I were standing by the door, he turned to Annie and said, "Your dad's neat, Annie—what a neat cab!" I could have kissed him.

We drove all through Brooklyn and up into Queens that afternoon, and then back down through Central Park, and the whole time Mr. Kenyon and his mother told stories about Italy, and Mrs. Kenyon laughed and prompted them. Mr. Kenyon's father, who had died in California, had been a butcher in his village in Sicily, and cats used to follow him all over because he fed them scraps. That was why the Kenyons still had cats; Mr. Kenyon said life just didn't seem right without a cat or two around. Chad was right that he was neat.

I can't really remember what Annie and I did during the next couple of days of vacation. Walked a lot—the Village, Chinatown, places like that. It's Sunday that's important to remember.

It's Sunday that I've been thinking around the edges of . . .

Have you ever felt really close to someone? So close that you can't understand why you and the other person have two separate bodies, two separate skins? I think it was Sunday when that feeling began.

We'd been riding around on the subway, talking when it wasn't too noisy, and had ended up at Coney Island. It was so late in the season that it was deserted, and very cold. We looked at all the closed-for-winter rides, and at a few straggling booth owners who were putting battered pastel-painted boards up over their popcorn or dime-toss or win-a-doll stands, and we bought hot dogs at Nathan's. There were only a couple of grubby old men eating there, I guess because most people don't have room even for Nathan's the weekend after Thanksgiving. Then we walked on the empty beach and joked about hiking all around the edge of Brooklyn up into Queens. We did manage to get pretty far, actually, at least well away from the deserted booths, and we found an old pier sort of thing with a lot of rotting brown pilings holding back some rocks—I guess it was more or less a breakwater—and we sat down, close together because it was so cold.

I remember that for a while there was a seagull wheeling around above our heads, squawking, but then it flew off toward Sheepshead Bay.

I'm not sure why we were so quiet, except that we knew school would start again for both of us the next day, and we wouldn't be able to meet so often or so easily. I had my senior project, and student council if I was reelected, and Annie had to rehearse for her recital. But we'd already worked out which days during the week we'd be able to see each other, and of course there would still be weekends, so maybe that wasn't why we were so quiet after all . . .

Mostly it was the closeness. It made my throat ache, wanting to speak of it.

I remember we were both watching the sun slowly go down over one end of the beach, making the sky to the west pink and yellow. I remember the water lapping gently against the pilings and the shore, and a candy wrapper—Three Musketeers, I think—blowing along the beach. Annie shivered.

Without thinking, I put my arm across her shoulders to warm her, and then before either of us knew what was happening, our arms were around each other and Annie's soft and gentle mouth was kissing mine.

When we did realize what was happening, we pulled away from each other, and Annie looked out over the water and I looked at the candy wrapper. It had gotten beyond the pilings by then, and was caught against a rock. For something to do, I walked over and stuffed it into my pocket, and then I stayed there, looking out over the water too, trying to keep my mind blank. I remember wishing the wind would literally blow through me, cold and pure and biting.

"Liza," Anne called in a quiet voice. "Liza, please come back."

Part of me didn't want to. But part of me did, and that part won.

Annie was digging a little hole in one crumbling piling with her fingernail.

"You'll break your nail," I said, and she looked up at me and smiled. Her eyes were soft and troubled and a little scared, but her mouth went on smiling, and then the wind blew her hair in wisps across my face and I had to move away.

She put her hand on mine, barely touching it. "It's all right with me," she whispered, "if it is with you."

"I—I don't know," I said.

It was like a war inside me; I couldn't even recognize all the sides. There was one that said, "No, this is wrong; you know it's wrong and bad and sinful," and there was another that said, "Nothing has ever felt so right and natural and true and good," and another that said it was happening too fast, and another that just wanted to stop thinking altogether and fling my arms around Annie and hold her forever. There were other sides, too, but I couldn't sort them out.

"Liza," Annie was saying, "Liza, I—I've wondered. I mean, I wondered if this might be happening. Didn't you?"

I shook my head. But somewhere inside I knew I had at least been confused.

Annie pulled her collar up around her throat and I wanted to touch her skin where the collar met it. It was as if I'd always wanted to touch her there but hadn't known it.

"It's my fault," Annie said softly. "I—I've thought sometimes, even before I met you, I mean, that I might be gay." She said the word "gay" easily, as if it were familiar to her, used that way.

"No," I managed to say, "no—it's not anyone's fault." I know that underneath my numbness I felt it made sense about me, too, but I couldn't think about it, or concentrate on it, not then.

Annie turned around and looked at me and the sadness in her eyes made me want to put my arms around her. "I'll go, Liza," she said, standing up. "I—I don't want to hurt you. I don't think you want this, so I *have* hurt you and, oh, God, Liza," she said, touching my face, "I don't want to, I—like you so much. I told you, you make me feel— real, more real than I've ever thought I could feel, more alive, you—you're better than a hundred Californias, but it's not only that, it's . . . ."

"Better than all those white birds?" I said around the ache that was in my throat again. "Because you're better than anything or anyone for me, too, Annie, better than— oh, I don't know better than what—better than every-thing—but that's not what I want to be saying—you— you're—Annie, I think I love you."

I heard myself say it as if I were someone else, but the moment the words were out, I knew more than I'd ever known anything that they were true.

94

Dear Annie,

*I've just been remembering Thanksgiving vacation,
and the beach near Coney Island. Annie, it makes me
ache for you, it . . .*

Liza crumpled the letter, then smoothed it out again,
tore it to shreds, and went outside.

She walked beside the Charles River in the cold. The
air was brittle with the coming winter; one sailboat strug-
gled against the biting wind. The guy in that boat's crazy,
she thought absently; his sail will freeze, his hands will
stick to the mainsheet and they'll have to pry him loose . . .

Annie, she thought, the name driving everything else
away, Annie, Annie . . .

8

School seemed strange the Monday after Thanksgiving. In a way it was nice to be back because it was familiar —but it also seemed irrelevant, as if I'd grown up and school was now part of my childhood.

I was almost surprised to see the ballot box in the main hall, and kids dropping folded pieces of paper in it. It wasn't that I'd really forgotten the election; it was just that it was part of my old world, too, and it had lost a lot of its importance. So I was quite calm when after lunch we were all told to report to the Lower School gym, which doubled as an auditorium, for "a few announcements."

Ms. Baxter gave me a big cheerful smile, I suppose to be forgiving and encouraging, but Mrs. Poindexter, in a purple dress I'd never seen before, her glasses dangling, looked grim. "I must've won," I quipped to Sally. "Look at her— she looks as if she's swallowed a cactus."

But Sally didn't laugh. In fact, I soon realized she must be nervous about something, because she kept licking her lips and she was clutching a couple of index cards, shuffling them around, picking at the corners.

"Ladies and gentlemen," said Mrs. Poindexter—her usual way of addressing large groups of us—"I have two announcements. The first and briefer one is that Eliza Winthrop will continue as head of student council."

There was quite a bit of applause, and school began mattering more to me again.

"And the second," Mrs. Poindexter said, holding up her hand for silence, "is that Walter Shander and Sally Jarrell have very kindly agreed to be student chairpeople for our fund-raising drive. Sally has a few words to say. Sally?"

Sally got up, still fidgeting nervously with her index cards.

"Well, I just want to say," she piped, "that I realized over Thanksgiving what a terrible thing I—I did with the ear piercing and all, and Walt and I talked over what I could do to make it up to the school, and then this morning Ms. Baxter said Mrs. Poindexter wanted students to get involved in the campaign. And so then I thought I could do that, and Walt said he'd help. I—I really want to make up to everyone for what I did, and this way, if anyone on the outside finds out about it, the ear infections, I mean, it'll be easier for Mrs. Poindexter and everyone to say that I'm really sorry . . ."

I swallowed against the sick feeling that was creeping up my throat from my stomach. It wasn't that I didn't think it was a nice thing for Sally to do—I did—it was that she seemed to be doing it for the wrong reasons.

"If the campaign's a success," she was saying, "that means that Foster can go on giving people a good education. Later, Walt and I will tell you about some dances and rallies and things we're planning, but right now I wanted first of all to apologize, and secondly—well, to ask for your support in the campaign." She blushed and ran back to her seat. There was applause again, but this time it was uncertain, as if the other kids were as surprised and as uncomfortable as I was about Sally's making so much of the ear piercing—she made it sound as if she thought she'd murdered someone.

But Mrs. Poindexter and Ms. Baxter looked like a couple of Cheshire cats, one large and one small.

"How was I?" Sally asked.

"Great, baby, terrific," Walt said, hugging her. "Wasn't she great, Liza?"

"Sure," I said, not wanting to hurt anyone's feelings.

After school I went to the art studio to do some work on my senior project. Sally and Walt were there, bent over a huge piece of poster board, painting, and I had to admit that Sally looked happier and more relaxed than I'd seen her for some time. Maybe, I thought, doing this won't be so bad for her after all.

"Hi, Liza," Walt called cheerfully, as I rummaged in the supply cabinet. "What shall we put you down for? We're making a list—how much do you think you can pledge?"

"Pledge?" I asked, not understanding.

"That's the word Mr. Piccolo says fund raisers use," Sally said proudly. "It means, how much do you promise to give to the Foster Fund Drive. Doesn't that sound good, Liza—Foster Fund Drive? So—um—metaphoric."

"Alliterative," I grumbled, sitting down.

"Welcome back, Liza," Ms. Stevenson said, peering out

from behind her easel, where she was working, as usual, on what we all jokingly called her masterpiece; it was a large abstract painting none of us understood.

"Thanks," I said, poking a pair of dividers down so hard I made a hole in my paper.

"Ms. Stevenson's pledged twenty-five dollars," Sally said sweetly, waving a small notebook.

"I don't know what I can give yet, Sally, okay?" I told her.

"Okay, okay," she snapped. "You don't have to be that way about it." Then her angry expression vanished as if it had been erased, and she got up and put her hand on my shoulder. "Oh, Liza, I'm sorry," she moaned. "It's me who shouldn't have been that way. I'm sorry I snapped at you for being uncertain." She patted my shoulder.

Ms. Baxter, I thought; she's been talking to Ms. Baxter —that's what it is.

But of course I couldn't say that. "It's okay," I muttered, glancing at Walt, who shrugged.

Ms. Stevenson dropped a large tube of zinc white, and Sally and Walt nearly crashed into each other trying to be first to pick it up for her.

I pushed away from the drawing table, muttered something about homework, and ran out of the art studio. Before I even thought about it consciously, I was in the phone booth in the basement, dialing Annie's number. As I waited for someone to answer, I reluctantly noticed the paint peeling off the steam pipes that ran along the walls, and a big crack that ran from the ceiling almost to the floor. *All right, all right*, I said silently. *I'll do something for the silly campaign!*

"Hello?" came Nana's gentle voice.

"Hi," I said—I never knew whether to call her Nana to her face or not. "This is Liza—is Annie there?"

"Hello, Lize. Yes, Annie's here. How you been? When you come see us?"

"I'm fine," I said, suddenly nervous. "I'll come soon."

"Okay. You not forget. Just a minute, I call Annie."

I could hear her calling in the background, and was relieved to hear Annie answer, and I closed my eyes, trying to visualize her in her apartment, only it was the beach that came back to me, and I could feel myself starting to sweat. But it still made sense to me; every time that scene came back to me, it made sense.

"Hi, Liza," came Annie's voice, sounding glad.

"Hi." I laughed for no reason I could think of. "I don't know why I'm calling you," I said, "except this has been a weird day and you're the only part of my life that seems sane."

"Did you get it?"

"Get what?"

"Oh, Liza! Did you get reelected?"

"Oh—that." It seemed about as far away as Mars, and about as important. "Yes, I got it."

"I'm so glad!" She paused, then said, "Liza, I . . ." and stopped.

"What?"

"I was going to say that I missed you all day. And I kept wondering about the election, and . . ."

"I missed you, too," I heard myself saying.

"Liza?"

I felt my heart speed up again, and my hands were

damp; I rubbed them on my jeans and tried to concentrate on the crack in the wall.

"Liza—are you—are you sorry? You know, about—you know."

"About Sunday?" I realized I was twisting the phone cord and tried to straighten it out again. I also noticed a bunch of juniors coming down the hall toward the phone booth, laughing and jostling each other. I closed my eyes to make them go away, to stay alone with Annie. "No," I said. "I'm not sorry. Confused, maybe. I—I keep trying not to think much about it. But . . ."

"I wrote you a dumb letter," Annie said softly. "But I didn't mail it."

"Do I get to see it?"

She hesitated, then said, "Sure. Come on up—can you?"

I didn't even look at my watch before I said, "Yes."

It was cold and very damp outside, as if it were going to snow, but it was warm in Annie's room. She had some quiet music on her rickety old-fashioned phonograph, and her hair was in two braids, which by now I knew usually meant she hadn't had time to wash it or that she'd been doing something active or messy, like helping her mother clean.

We just looked at each other for a minute there in the doorway of her room, as if neither of us knew what to say or how to act with each other. But I felt myself leave Sally and school and the fund-raising drive behind me, the way a cicada leaves its shell when it turns from an immature grub into its almost grown-up self.

Annie took my hand shyly, pulled me into her room, and shut the door. "Hi," she said.

I felt myself smiling, wanting to laugh with pleasure at seeing her, but also needing to laugh out of nervousness, I guess. "Hi."

Then we both did laugh, like a couple of idiots, standing there awkwardly looking at each other.

And we both moved at the same time into each other's arms, hugging. It was just a friendly hug at first, an I'm-so-glad-to-see-you hug. But then I began to be very aware of Annie's body pressed against mine and of feeling her heart beat against my breast, so I moved away.

"Sorry," she said, turning away also.

I touched her shoulder; it was rigid. "No—no, don't be."

"You moved away so fast."

"I—Annie, please."

"Please what?"

"Please—I don't know. Can't we just be . . ."

"Friends?" she said, whirling around. "Just friends—wonderful stock phrase, isn't it? Only what you said on the beach was—was . . ." She turned away again, covering her face with her hands.

"Annie," I said miserably, "Annie, Annie. I—I do love you, Annie." There, I thought. That's the second time I've said it.

Annie groped on her desk-table and handed me an envelope. "I'm sorry," she said. "I didn't get any sleep last night and—well, I couldn't tell you a single thing anyone said in school today, even at rehearsal. I'm going to wash my face."

I nodded, trying to smile at her as if everything was all right—there's no reason, I remember thinking, why it shouldn't be—and I sat down on the edge of Annie's bed and opened the letter.

Dear Liza,

It's three-thirty in the morning and this is the fifth time I've tried to write this to you. Someone said something about three o'clock in the morning being the dark night of the soul—something like that. That's true, at least for this three o'clock and this soul.

Look, I have to be honest—I want to try to be, anyhow. I told you about Beverly because I knew at that point that I loved you. I was trying to warn you, I guess. As I said, I've wondered for a long time if I was gay. I even tried to prove I wasn't, last summer with a boy, but it was ridiculous.

I know you said on the beach that you think you love me, and I've been trying to hold on to that, but I'm still scared that if I told you everything about how I feel, you might not be ready for it. Maybe you've already felt pressured into thinking you have to feel the same way, out of politeness, sort of, because you like me and don't want to hurt my feelings. The thing is, since you haven't thought about it—about being gay—I'm trying to tell myself very firmly that it wouldn't be fair of me to—I don't know, influence you, try to push you into something you don't want, or don't want yet, or something.

Liza, I think what I'm saying is that, really, if you don't want us to see each other any more, it's okay.

Love,
Annie

I stood there holding the letter and looking at the word "Love" at the end of it, knowing that I was jealous of the boy Annie'd mentioned, and that my not seeing Annie any more would be as ridiculous for me as she said her experiment with the boy had been for her.

Could I even begin an experiment like that, I wondered, startled; would I?

It was true I'd never consciously thought about being gay. But it also seemed true that if I were, that might pull together not only what had been happening between me and Annie all along and how I felt about her, but also a lot of things in my life before I'd known her—things I'd never let myself think about much. Even when I was little, I'd often felt as if I didn't quite fit in with most of the people around me; I'd felt isolated in some way that I never understood. And as I got older—well, in the last two or three years, I'd wondered why I'd rather go to the movies with Sally or some other girl than with a boy, and why, when I imagined living with someone someday, permanently I mean, that person was always female.

I read Annie's letter again, and again felt how ridiculous not seeing her any more would be—how much I'd miss her, too.

When Annie came back from the bathroom, she stood across the room watching me for a few minutes. I could tell she was trying very hard to pretend her letter didn't matter, but her eyes were so bright that I was pretty sure they were wet.

"I'd tear this up," I said finally, "if it weren't for the fact that it's the first letter you've ever written me, and so I want to keep it."

"Oh, Liza!" she said softly, not moving. "Are you sure?"

I felt my face getting hot and my heart speeding up again. Annie's eyes were so intent on mine, it was as if we were standing with no distance between us—but there was the whole room.

I think I nodded, and I know I held out my hand. I felt about three years old.

She took my hand, and then she touched my face. "I still don't want to rush you," she said softly. "I—it scares me, too, Liza. I—I just recognize it more, maybe."

"Right now I just want to feel you close to me," I said, or something like it, and in a few minutes we were lying down on Annie's bed, holding each other and sometimes kissing, but not really touching. Mostly just being happy.

Still scared, though, too.

9

That winter, all Annie had to do was walk into a room or appear at a bus stop or a corner where we were meeting and I didn't even have to think about smiling; I could feel my face smiling all on its own. We saw each other every afternoon that we could, and on weekends, and called each other just about every night, and even that didn't seem enough; sometimes we even arranged to call each other from pay phones at lunchtime. It was a good thing I'd never had much trouble with schoolwork, because I floated through classes, writing letters to Annie or daydreaming. The fund-raising campaign went on around me without my paying much attention to it. I did pledge some money; I listened to Sally and Walt make speeches; I even helped them collect pledges from some of the other kids—but I was never really there, because Annie filled my mind. Songs I heard on the radio suddenly seemed to fit Annie and me; poems I read seemed written especially for us— we began sending each other poems that we liked. I would have gone broke buying Annie plants if I hadn't known how much it bothered her that I often had money and she usually didn't.

We kept finding new things about New York to show

each other; it was as if we were both seeing the city for the first time. One afternoon I suddenly noticed, and then showed Annie, how the sunlight dripped over the ugly face of her building, softening it and making it glow almost as if there were a mysterious light source hidden inside its drab walls. And Annie showed me how ailanthus trees grow under subway and sewer gratings, stretching toward the sun, making shelter in the summer, she said, laughing, for the small dragons that live under the streets. Much of that winter was—magical is the only word again —and a big part of that magic was that no matter how much of ourselves we found to give each other, there was always more we wanted to give.

One Saturday in early December we got our parents to agree to let us go out to dinner together. "Why shouldn't we?" Annie had said to me—it was her idea. "People go out for dinner on dates and stuff, don't they?" She grinned and said formally, "Liza Winthrop, I'd like to make a date with you for dinner. I know this great Italian restaurant . . ."

It was a great Italian restaurant. It was in the West Village, and tiny, with no more than ten or twelve tables, and the ones along the wall, where we sat, were separated by iron scrollwork partitions, so we had the illusion of privacy if not privacy itself. It was dark, too; our main light came from a candle in a Chianti bottle. Annie's face looked golden and soft, like the face of a woman in a Renaissance painting.

"What's this?" I asked, pointing to a long name on the menu and trying to resist the urge to touch Annie's lovely face. "*Scapeloni al Marsala?*"

Annie's laugh was as warm as the candlelight. "No, no," she corrected. "*Scaloppine. Scaloppine alla Marsala.*"

"*Scaloppine alla Marsala,*" I repeated. "What is it?"

"It's veal," she said. "*Vitello.* Sort of like thin veal cutlets, in a wonderful sauce."

"Is it good?" I asked—but I was still thinking of the way she'd said *vitello*, with a musical pause between the *l*'s.

Annie laughed again and kissed the closed fingers of her right hand. Then she popped her fingers open and tossed her hand up in a cliché but airy gesture that came straight out of a movie about Venice we'd seen the week before. "Is it good!" she said. "Nana makes it."

So we both had *scaloppine alla Marsala*, after an antipasto and along with a very illegal half bottle of wine, and then Annie convinced me to try a wonderful pastry called *cannoli*, and after that we had *espresso*.

And still we sat there, with no one asking us to leave. We stayed so late that both my parents and Annie's were furious when we got home. "You never call any more, Liza," my father said, muttering something about wishing I'd see other people besides Annie. "I don't want to set a curfew," he said, "but two girls wandering around New York at night—it just isn't safe."

Dad was right, but time with Annie was real time stopped, and more and more often, we both forgot to call.

Chad kept kidding me that I was in love, and asking with whom, and then Sally and Walt did, too, and after a while I didn't even mind, because even if they had the wrong idea about it, they were right. Soon it wasn't hard any more to say it—to myself, I mean, as well as over and over again to Annie—and to accept her saying it to me.

We touched each other more easily—just kissed or held hands or hugged each other, though—nothing more than that. We didn't really talk much about being gay; most of the time we just talked about ourselves. *We* were what seemed important then, not some label.

The day the first snow fell was a Saturday and Annie and I called each other up at exactly the same moment, over and over again, tying up our phones with busy signals for ten minutes. I don't remember which of us got through first, but around an hour later we were both running through Central Park like a couple of maniacs, making snow angels and pelting each other with snowballs. We even built a fort with the help of three little boys and their big brother, who was our age, and after that we all bought chestnuts and pretzels and sat on a bench eating them till the boys had to go home. Some of the chestnuts were rotten. I remember that because Annie said, throwing one away, "It's the first sign of a dying city—rotten chestnuts." I could even laugh at that, along with the boys, because I knew that the ugly things about New York weren't bothering her so much any more.

Annie and I went ice skating a few times, and we tried to get our parents to let us go to Vermont to ski, but they wouldn't. Mr. Kenyon took us and Nana and Annie's mother out to Westchester in his cab just before Christmas to look at the lights on people's houses, and they all wished me *"Buon Natale"* when they dropped me off at home. On Christmas afternoon, I gave Annie a ring.

"Oh, Liza," she said, groping in the pocket of her coat; we were on the Promenade, and it had just begun to snow. "Look!"

Out of her pocket she took a little box the same size as the little box I'd just handed her.

I looked around for people and then kissed the end of her nose; it was almost dark, and besides, I didn't really care if anyone saw us. "Is the silly grin on my face," I asked her, "as silly as the silly grin on your face?"

"Jerk," she said. "Open your present."

"You first."

"I can't, my hands are shaking. You know what happens to my gloves if I take them off."

"What happens to your gloves if you take them off is you lose them. But you don't lose them if you give them to me." I held out my hand. "I'll hold your gloves, Unicorn, okay?"

"Okay, okay," she said, and stripped them off and fumbled with the metallic ribbon on the box with a wonderful clumsiness that I have never seen anyone else as graceful as Annie have.

"Oh, for God's sake," I said. "I'll bite it off if it's stuck!"

"You will not! It's my first Christmas present from you and I'm going to keep every scrap of it forever, ribbon and all—oh, Liza!"

By then she had the box open and was staring down at the little gold ring with the pale blue stone that I'd found in an antique shop on Atlantic Avenue, at the edge of Brooklyn Heights.

"Liza, Liza," she said, looking at me—no, staring—with wonder. "I don't believe this." She nodded toward the box I was holding. "Open yours."

I gave Annie back her gloves and stuffed my own into my pockets, and I opened the box she had handed me and found a gold ring with a pale green stone—no, not identical to the ring I'd given her, but almost.

"I don't believe it either," I said. "But I also do."

"It's some kind of sign."

"Come on."

"It is, Liza; you know it is."

"The occult sciences," I said, intentionally pompous, "are the only ones that would even attempt to explain this kind of coincidence, and the occult sciences are not . . ."

Annie flung her arms around my neck and kissed me, even though there were four kids galloping down the snowy path from Clark Street to the Promenade, showering each other with snowballs.

"If you don't put that ring on this minute, I'm going to take it back," Annie whispered in my ear. "Occult sciences, indeed!" She leaned back, looking at me, her hands still on my shoulders, her eyes shining softly at me and snow falling, melting, on her nose. *"Buon Natale,"* she whispered, *"amore mio."*

"Merry Christmas, my love," I answered.

My parents and Chad and I went up to Annie's school to hear her recital, which had been postponed till right after Christmas because of snow. Annie had said many times that the only decent teacher in the whole school was her music teacher and the only department, even counting phys. ed., that tried to do anything with extra-curricular activities was the music department. As soon as I heard Annie sing that night, I could see why a music department would give recitals as long as Annie was around to be in them.

Hearing Annie sing in the recital was nothing like hearing her sing in the museum that first day, or hearing her hum around her apartment or mine or on the street the way I had a few times since then. I knew she had a lovely voice, and I knew from the time in the museum that she could put a lot of feeling behind what she sang—but this was more than all those things combined. The other kids in the recital were good—maybe the way I'd expected Annie to be—but right before Annie sang, she looked out at the audience as if to say, "Listen, there's this really beautiful song I'd like you to hear"—as if she wanted to make the audience a present of it. The audience seemed to know something unusual was coming, for when Annie looked at them, they settled back, calm and happy and expectant, and when she started singing, you couldn't even hear anyone breathe. I glanced at Dad and Mom and Chad to see if maybe it was my loving Annie that made me think she was so good, but I could see from their faces, and from the faces of the other people—not just her family, who looked about ready to burst with pride—that everyone else thought she was as good as I did.

I'm not sure how to describe Annie's voice, or if anyone really could, except maybe a music critic. It's a low soprano—mezzo-soprano is its technical name—and it's a little husky—not gravelly husky, but rich—and, according to my mother, it's one hundred percent on pitch all the time. It's also almost perfectly in control; when Annie wants to fill a room with her voice, she can, but she can also make it as soft as a whisper, a whisper you can always hear.

But none of that was what made the audience sit there

not moving every time Annie sang. It was the feeling again, the same thing that first drew me to Annie in the museum, only much, much more so. Annie's singing was so spontaneous, and she gave so much of herself, that it sounded as if she'd actually written each song, or was making each one up as she went along, the way she'd done in the museum. When she sang something sad, I wanted to cry; when she sang something happy, I felt myself smiling. Dad said he felt the same, and Mom had a long serious talk with Annie the next afternoon about becoming a professional—but Annie said she wasn't sure yet if she wanted to, although she knew she wanted to major in music and continue singing no matter what else she did. Chad, even though he was shy with girls, gave her a big hug after the performance and said, "There's nothing to say, Annie, you were so good."

I couldn't think of anything to say, either. Mostly I just wanted to put my arms around her, but at the same time I felt in awe of her—this was a whole new Annie, an Annie I hardly knew. I don't remember what I did or said —squeezed her hand, I think, and said something lame. But she said later that she didn't care what anyone thought except me.

I had the flu that winter, badly, some time late in January, I think it was. The night before, I was fine, but the next morning I woke up with my throat on fire and my head feeling as if a team of Clydesdales were galloping through it. Mom made me go back to bed and came in every couple of hours with something for me to drink. I think the only reason I remember the doctor's making one of his rare house calls is because I nearly choked on the pills that Mom gave me to take after he'd left.

Some time that first afternoon, though, I heard voices outside my door. Mom had let Chad wave to me from the threshold earlier, and it was too early for Dad to be home, so I knew it couldn't be either of them. And then Annie was beside me, with Mom protesting from the door.

"It's okay, Mrs. Winthrop," she was saying. "I had the flu this year already."

"Liar," I whispered, when Mom finally left.

"Last year, this year," said Annie, turning the cloth on my head to its cooler side. "It's all the same." She put her hand on my cheek. "You must feel rotten."

"Not so much rotten," I said, "as not here. As if I were floating, very far away. I don't want to be far away from you," I said, reaching for her hand, "but I am." I really must have been pretty sick, because I could barely concentrate, even on Annie.

Annie held my hand, stroking it softly. "Don't talk," she said. "I won't let you float away. You can't go far with me holding on to you. I'll keep you here, love, shh." She began to sing very softly and sweetly, and although I was still floating, I was riding on clouds now, with Annie's voice and her hand gently anchoring me to Earth.

We didn't always use words when we were together; we didn't need to. That was uncanny, but maybe the best thing of all, although I don't think we thought about it much; it just happened. There's a Greek legend—no, it's in something Plato wrote—about how true lovers are really two halves of the same person. It says that people wander around searching for their other half, and when they find him or her, they are finally whole and perfect. The thing that gets me is that the story says that originally all people were really pairs of people, joined back to back, and that some of the pairs were man and man, some woman and woman, and others man and woman. What happened was that all of these double people went to war with the gods, and the gods, to punish them, split them all in two. That's why some lovers are heterosexual and some are homosexual, female and female, or male and male.

I loved that story when I first heard it—in junior year, I think it was—because it seemed fair, and right, and sensible. But that winter I really began to believe it was true, because the more Annie and I learned about each other, the more I felt she was the other half of me.

The oddest thing, perhaps, was that even as the winter went on, we still didn't touch each other much more than we had at the beginning, after around Christmas, I mean.

But we did realize more and more that winter that we wanted to—I especially realized it, I guess, since it was so new to me.

And the more we realized it, the more we tried to avoid it.

No. The more I did, at least at first . . .

We were in Annie's room; her parents were out and Nana was asleep; we were listening to an opera on the radio, and we were sitting on the floor. My head was in Annie's lap, and her hand was on my hair, moving softly to my throat, then to my breast—and I sat up and reached for the radio, fiddling with the dial, saying something dumb like, "The volume's fading," which it wasn't . . .

We were in my kitchen; my parents and Chad were in the living room watching TV; Annie had stayed for dinner and we were doing the dishes. I put my arms around her from behind and held her body so close to mine that I wasn't sure whose pulse I felt throbbing. But when she turned to me, I reached quickly for the dish towel and a plate . . .

Then it began happening the other way around, too: Annie began moving away from me. I remember one time in the subway; it was pretty late, and for a minute there was no one in the car with us. So I leaned over and kissed Annie, and she stiffened, holding herself away from me, rigid . . .

The worst thing was that we were too shy to talk about it. And we got so tangled up that we began misunderstanding each other more and more often, just in general, and the wordless communication we prized so much weakened, and we began to fight about dumb things, like what time we were going to meet and what we were going to do, or whether Annie was coming to my apartment or I was going to hers, or if we should take the subway or the bus.

The worst fight was in March.

We'd gone to the museum, the Metropolitan, and Annie seemed to want to stay in front of the medieval choir screen forever, and I wanted to go to the Temple of Dendur.

"There's nothing to look at," I said nastily—she was just staring, at least that's what it looked like to me. "You must have memorized every curlicue by now. Really, how many of those post things are there?" I pointed to one of the hundreds of vertical shafts of which the screen is made.

Annie turned to me, blazing; I'd never seen her so angry. "Look, why don't you just go to your silly temple if you want to so much? Some people can pray better in the dark, that's all. But you probably don't pray at all, you're so pure and sure of everything."

A guard glanced in our direction, as if he were trying to decide whether to tell us to be quiet. We weren't talking loud yet, but we were getting there.

I was mad enough to ignore most of what Annie'd said till later. I just turned and walked away, past the guard, to the temple. I must have stayed there for a good half hour, until it hit me that I'd said the first rotten thing. But when I walked back to the choir screen, ready to apologize, Annie was gone.

"Did Annie call?" I asked casually when I got home around six-thirty.

"No," Mom said, giving me an odd look.

I don't think I said a word during dinner, and all evening I jumped every time the phone rang.

"Liza had a fight," Chad sang gleefully the third time I ran for the phone and had to turn it over to someone else—usually him. "H'm, Lize? Bet'cha you and Annie fought over some boy, huh? Or . . ."

"That will do, Chad," Mom said, looking at me. "Haven't you got homework?"

"If he hasn't, I have," I said, and fled to my room, slamming the door.

At about ten o'clock, when Chad was in the shower, I called Annie, but Nana said she'd gone to bed.

"Could you—could you see if she's still awake?" I asked humbly.

There was a pause and then Nana said, "Lize, you have a fight with Annie, no?"

"Yes," I admitted.

I could almost hear her head nodding. "I guess that when I see her come in. She look all fussed. Maybe you call tomorrow, eh? It's none of my business, but sometimes people just need a little time."

I knew she was right, but I couldn't let it go. I didn't want to go to sleep thinking Annie was mad at me, or that I'd hurt her in some unforgivable way.

"Could you—could you just tell her I'm sorry?" I said.

"Sure." Nana sounded relieved. "I tell her. But you hang up now. Call tomorrow, okay?"

"Okay," I said, hanging up.

Mom's hand was on my shoulder the moment I put down the receiver. "Liza," she began, "Liza, shouldn't we talk about this? You seem so upset, honey, what . . ."

But I wrenched away and ran back to my room, where I read until dawn, mostly Shakespeare's sonnets, and cried over the ones I had once copied out and sent to Annie.

The next afternoon I ran most of the way home from school, so I'd get there before Chad; I knew Mom had a meeting, and I wanted to be sure I was alone when I called Annie. But Annie was waiting outside my building, sitting on the steps in a heavy red-and-black lumber jacket I'd never seen before.

I was so surprised to see her I just stopped and stood there, but she got up right away and came toward me, her arms woodenly at her sides. The lumber jacket was so big it looked as though it belonged to someone else. "Want to go for a walk?" she asked. She looked haggard, as if she hadn't slept any more than I had.

I nodded and we walked silently toward the Promenade. I kept twisting Annie's ring with the thumb and little finger of the hand it was on, wondering if she was going to want it back.

Annie leaned against the railing, and seemed to be trying to follow the progress of the Staten Island ferry through the fog.

"Annie," I began finally, "Annie, I . . ."

She turned, leaning her back against the railing. "Nana told me you'd called and that you were sorry," she said. "Accepted. But . . ."

"But?" I said, my heart racing. She hadn't smiled yet, and I knew I hadn't either.

"But—" said Annie, turning back to face the harbor, soft hair blowing around her face. "Liza, we're like the temple and the choir screen, as I thought the day I met you, only then I was just guessing. You—you really are like the temple—light—you go happily on without really noticing, and I'm dark, like the choir screen, like the room it's in. I feel too much and want too much, I guess, and . . ." She turned to face me again; her eyes were desolate. "I want to be in the real world with you, Liza, for you, but—but we're still running away. Or you are, or —Liza, I don't want to be afraid of this, of—of the physical part of loving you. But you're making me afraid, and guilty, because you seem to think it's wrong, or dirty, or something—maybe you did all along, I don't know . . ."

"No!" I interrupted loudly, unable to keep still any longer. "No—not dirty, Annie, not . . . I don't want to make you afraid," I finished lamely.

For a minute Annie seemed to be waiting for me to say something else, but I couldn't just then. "I really was praying there in the museum," she said softly, "when you got so mad. I was praying that I could ignore it if you wanted me to—not the love, but the physical part of it. But having to do that—I think that makes me more afraid than facing it would."

It came crashing through my foggy mind that in spite of everything Annie had just said I wanted desperately to touch her, to hold her, and then I was able to speak again. "It's not true," I said carefully, "that I want to ignore it. And I'm not going on happily not noticing." I stopped, feeling Annie take my hand, and realized my fists were clenched. "It scares me, too, Annie," I managed to say, "but not because I think it's wrong or anything—at least I don't think it's that. It's—it's mostly because it's so strong, the love and the friendship and every part of it." I think that was when I finally realized that—as I said it.

"But you always move away," she said.

"You do, too."

"I—I know."

Then we both looked out at the harbor again, as if we'd just met and were shy with each other again.

But at least after that we were able to begin talking about it.

"It's timing, partly, it's as if we never want the same thing at the same time," I said.

We were sitting on the sofa in my parents' living room. My parents and Chad were out, but we didn't know for how long.

"I don't think so," said Annie. "It's the one thing we don't know about each other, the one thing we aren't letting each other know—as if we're blocking the channels, because—because we're so scared of it, Liza. The real question still is why." She reached for my hand. "I wish we could just sort of—let what happens happen," she said. "Without thinking so much about it."

Her thumb was moving gently on my hand; her eyes had a special soft look in them I've never seen in anyone's but Annie's, and only in Annie's when she looked at me. "I'll promise to try not to move away next time," she said.

"I—I'll promise, too," I said, my mouth so dry the words scraped. "Right now I don't think I could stop anything from happening that started."

But a few minutes later my father's key turned in the lock and we both jumped guiltily away from each other.

And that was when there began to be that problem, too —that there was really no place where we could be alone. Of course there were times when no one was home at Annie's apartment or mine, but we were always afraid that someone would walk in. And it wasn't long before we began using that fear to mask our deeper one; we were still restrained and hesitant with each other.

But maybe—and I think this is true—maybe we also just needed more time.

10

*F*inally the dreary cold winter warmed up and leaves
started bursting out on the trees. Daffodils and tulips and
those blue flowers that grow in clusters on stiff stems began
to pop up all over the Heights, and Annie and I spent
much more time outdoors, which helped a little. Annie dis-
covered more dooryard gardens—even on my own street—
than I ever thought existed. We managed to go for a lot of
walks that spring, even though Annie was very busy with
rehearsals for a new recital and I was trying to finish my
senior project and was helping Sally and Walt with the
fund drive—things really did look pretty bad for Foster.

Late one afternoon a week and a half before spring vacation, Mrs. Poindexter called me into her office.

"Eliza," she said, settling back into her brown chair and
actually almost smiling. "Eliza, I have been most pleased
with your conduct these last months. You have shown
none of the immaturity that steered you so wrongly last
fall; your grades have, as usual, been excellent, and Ms.
Baxter reports to me that you have at last begun to show
an interest in the fund drive. Needless to say, your record
is now clear."

"Mrs. Poindexter," I asked after I recovered from the
relief I felt, "is it true that Foster might have to close?"

Mrs. Poindexter gave me a long look. Then she sighed and said—gently—"I'm afraid it is, dear."

Mrs. Poindexter had never called anyone "dear" as far as I knew. Certainly never me.

"Eliza, you have been going to Foster since kindergarten. That's nearly thirteen years—almost your entire lifetime. Some of our teachers have been here much longer— I myself have been headmistress for twenty-five years."

"It would be awful," I said, suddenly feeling sorry for her, "if Foster had to close."

Mrs. Poindexter sniffed and fingered her glasses chain. "We have tried to make it the best possible school. We have never had the money to compete with schools like Brearley, but . . ." She smiled and reached out, patting my hand. "But this needn't concern you, although I appreciate your sympathy. What I need from you—what Foster needs from you," she said, squaring her shoulders, "is a heightened participation in the fund drive. You as student council president have enormous influence—a certain public influence as well, I may say. Or you could have, if you would use your position advantageously."

I licked my lips; if she was going to ask me to make speeches, I was going to have to use every bit of self-control I had not to say no. Making just the required campaign speeches after I was nominated for council president had been one of the hardest things I'd ever done. Even when I had to get up in front of English class and give an oral report, I always felt as if I were going to my execution.

"The fund drive," said Mrs. Poindexter, picking up her desk calendar, "must be speeded up—we have so little time now before the end of school. Mr. Piccolo and the fund raiser tell me we are still far short of our goal, and the recruitment campaign has not, so far, been a success. Mr. Piccolo says it is his feeling that interest will pick up in the spring, so there is hope." She smiled. "Eliza, I'm sure you will agree that this is the time for student council to take an active part, to lead the other students, to give Sally and Walt, who are working so very hard, a real boost, so to speak."

"Well," I said, "we could talk about it at the next meeting. But there isn't another, is there, till after vacation?"

"There is now," Mrs. Poindexter said triumphantly, pointing at the calendar with her glasses. "I have scheduled one—assuming of course that you and the others can go—but you will find that out for me, won't you, like my good right hand? I've scheduled a special council meeting for this Friday afternoon—and because Mr. Piccolo and his publicity committee will be using the Parlor for an emergency fund-drive meeting of their own, and because my apartment is too small and the school dining room seems inappropriate, I have asked Ms. Stevenson as student council adviser to volunteer her home, and she and Ms. Widmer have very kindly agreed." She leaned back, still smiling. "Isn't that kind of them?"

I just looked at her for a minute, not knowing which made me madder—her calling a council meeting without saying anything to me first, or her making Ms. Stevenson and Ms. Widmer "volunteer" to have it where they lived.

"You are free Friday afternoon, aren't you?"

For a second I was tempted to invent an unbreakable dentist appointment, but—well, if Foster's really in trouble, I thought, I can't very well go around throwing obstacles in its way. Besides, I felt pretty sure Mrs. Poindexter would go ahead with the meeting even if I weren't there.

"Yes," I said, trying not to say it too obviously through my teeth. "Sure, I'm free."

Mrs. Poindexter's smile broadened. "Good girl," she said. "And you will notify the others—or ask Mary Lou to do so? You shouldn't have to, actually, being the president . . ."

I think it was that last remark—her making a big deal of my being president after scheduling a meeting without even notifying me till afterwards—that made me storm over to the art studio.

Ms. Stevenson was washing brushes. "I've been working on the railroad," she sang softly above the sound of running water, "all the livelong day—hello, Liza. You been working on the railroad too?"

"If," I said, yanking out a chair and throwing myself down at one of the tables, "that's a subtle way of making a comment about being railroaded into a certain council meeting, yes, I sure have been. I just came from Mrs. Poindexter's office. Only the spikes got pounded into me instead of into the railroad ties. Or something. I don't know."

"Well," said Ms. Stevenson, carefully stroking a brush back and forth against her palm to see if the color was out of it yet, "I suppose I should point out that it's all for a good cause. We need Foster; now Foster needs us. Mrs. Poindexter means well, after all."

"I know," I said, sighing, more discouraged than before,

since Ms. Stevenson seemed so calm. "But dammit—sorry, darn it—it's the principle of the thing. She might have asked me first—or even just told me—and she might have asked to use your place instead of making you 'volunteer' it. Volunteer, hah!"

Ms. Stevenson laughed. "It was Ms. Baxter who asked, on Mrs. Poindexter's behalf. I don't think she enjoyed doing it, though. I don't think she quite approves of students going to teachers' homes."

"I should think she'd love it," I grumbled. "Disciples at one's feet and all that."

"Cheer up, Liza," Ms. Stevenson said. "Except I warn you the feet part will probably be true. We don't have all that many chairs."

"Don't you mind at all?" I asked incredulously. "Doesn't Ms. Widmer mind? She's not even on council. I mean, weren't you even mad that Mrs. Poindexter just—just up and ordered the whole thing? Council's supposed to be democratic for—for Pete's sake!"

Ms. Stevenson's face crinkled around her eyes. "Mind?" she said, pointing to the wastebasket, which I now saw was a quarter full of crumpled scraps of paper with angry-looking writing all over them. "The one thing that having a temper has taught me, Liza," she said, "is that most of the time it's better to do one's exploding in private. But the thing is, we do have to remember that she *is* the headmistress, and she *has* done a lot for the school for many, many years, and—oh, blast it, Liza, not everyone can be as true to all the principles of democracy as you and I, can they?"

Well, that made me laugh, which made me feel a little better.

But I wonder if Ms. Stevenson would be quite so understanding of Mrs. Poindexter now as she was then.

None of us had ever been to Ms. Stevenson's and Ms. Widmer's house before—well, maybe Mrs. Poindexter had, or Ms. Baxter, but none of the kids had. Their house was in Cobble Hill, which is separated from Brooklyn Heights by Atlantic Avenue. Cobble Hill used to be considered a "bad" neighborhood; my mother never let me and Chad cross Atlantic when we were little—but I don't think it was ever that bad. People have fixed up a lot of the houses there now, and it's a nice mixture of nationalities and ages and kinds of jobs. Unpretentious, I guess you could call it—something the Heights tries to be but isn't.

The house where Ms. Stevenson and Ms. Widmer lived was just that—a house—which is unusual in New York, where most people live in apartments. It's a town house, attached to a lot of other houses, so it's technically part of a row house. There are two long row houses, containing ten or so town houses each, facing one another across a wonderfully tangled private garden. Ms. Baxter, Ms. Stevenson told us that day, lived on the other side of the garden, and about three doors down. Behind each set of houses was a cobblestone strip with separate little garden areas, one per tenant. Everyone's back door opened onto that strip, so people sat outside a lot and talked. Everyone was very friendly.

The special council meeting was the afternoon of the night of Annie's spring recital, and she was resting, so I went right down to Cobble Hill after school. I was the first to arrive. Ms. Stevenson and Ms. Widmer showed me around and kidded me about my "professional interest" in the house. There were three floors. I didn't see the top one, where the bedrooms were, but I saw both the others—basically two rooms per floor, and very cozy. The bottom floor had the kitchen, which was huge and bright, with gleaming white-flecked-with-black linoleum, copper-colored appliances, and dark wood cabinets. The back door, leading out to the cobblestones and the garden, was off that. There was a tiny bathroom off the kitchen and a little hall at the foot of the stairs, with a bare brick wall covered with hanging plants. The dining room was off that, with more exposed brick and a heavy-beamed ceiling. "This is our cave," Ms. Widmer said, showing it to me. "Especially in winter when it's dark at dinnertime." I could see that it would be cavelike, because of the heavy low beams and the little window. Also, the ground was higher at the front of the house than at the back, dropping the dining room below ground level so its window looked out on people's feet as they passed by. Two of the walls were lined with books, which added to the cavelike atmosphere.

Upstairs on the second floor were the living room and a sort of study or workroom. A steep flight of steps led from the front garden area to the front door, which led directly into the study. There was an old-fashioned mail slot in the door, and I thought how much nicer and more private that must be than getting one's mail from a locked box in the entryway as we did. "Here's where your fates are decided." Ms. Widmer laughed, pointing to the pile of papers on her desk, topped with her roll book. Ms. Stevenson had an easel set up near the window, and art supplies neatly arranged on a shelf against the wall.

The living room was on the other side of the stairwell, comfortable and cozy like the rest of the house. There were lots of plants around, records and books everywhere, nice pictures on the walls—many of them, Ms. Stevenson said, done by former students—and two enormous cats, one black and one orange, who followed us everywhere and of course made me think of Annie and of her grandfather, the butcher.

"I don't know what we're going to do with them this spring vacation," Ms. Widmer said when I stooped to pat one of the cats after I'd told her and Ms. Stevenson about Annie's grandfather. "We're going away, and the boy who usually takes care of them is also."

I'm not as fond of cats as Annie is, but I certainly like them, and I knew I wouldn't mind being able to spend a little more time in that house. "I could feed the cats," I heard myself say.

Ms. Stevenson and Ms. Widmer exchanged a look, and Ms. Stevenson asked how much money I'd want and I told her whatever they gave the boy. They said a dollar-fifty a day, and I said fine. Then the other kids began arriving for the meeting.

It was funny, being in their house and seeing them as people as well as teachers. For instance, Ms. Stevenson lit a cigarette at one point, and I nearly fell off my chair. It had never occurred to me that she smoked, because of course she couldn't at school except in the Teachers' Room, the way seniors could in the Senior Lounge. Later she told me she'd tried to quit once, because it had begun to make her hoarse, which wasn't good for her singing in the chorus or for coaching the debate team. But she'd gained so much weight and had been in such a rotten mood all the time that she'd decided it would be kinder to other people as well as to herself to go back to it.

I'd never thought much about Ms. Stevenson's and Ms. Widmer's living in the same house, and I don't think many other people at school had either, but that afternoon it seemed to me that they'd probably been living together for quite a long time. They seemed to own everything jointly; you didn't get the idea that the sofa belonged to one of them and the armchair to the other or anything like that. And they seemed so comfortable with each other. Not that they seemed uncomfortable at school, but at school they were rarely together except at special events like plays or dances, which they usually helped chaperone. Even then, they were usually with a whole bunch of other teachers, and Sally had always said that at dances one or the other of them was usually whirling around the floor with one of the men teachers.

But in their house they were like a couple of old shoes, each with its own special lumps and bumps and cracks, but nonetheless a pair that fit with ease into the same shoe box.

"It's so nice of you two to have us here," said Mrs. Poindexter when we were all more or less settled in the living room and Ms. Widmer and Ms. Stevenson were passing out Cokes and tea and cookies. "All" not only included members of the student council but also Sally and Walt as Student Fund Drive Chairpeople, and Ms. Baxter as well. Ms. Baxter was taking notes, which made Mary Lou furious.

Mrs. Poindexter was wearing a black dress with little bits of white lace at the throat and wrists that reminded me of Ms. Baxter's handkerchiefs. Somehow it made her look as if she were about to bury someone.

"I will read," she said, "with apologies to Sally and Walt, who have already seen it, from Mr. Piccolo's last report to me. Ms. Baxter?" She settled her glasses onto her nose.

"Mrs. Poindexter," said Ms. Stevenson as Ms. Baxter pulled a file folder out of the chunky, old-fashioned brief-case she'd brought with her, "shouldn't the meeting be called to order first?"

Mrs. Poindexter flipped her glasses down. "Oh, very well," she said crossly. "The meeting . . ."

Ms. Stevenson cleared her throat.

"Eliza," said Mrs. Poindexter smoothly, "we're waiting."

"The meeting," I said as steadily as possible, "will come to order. The chair"—I couldn't help giving that word a little extra emphasis—"recognizes Mrs. Poindexter."

Mrs. Poindexter crashed her glasses back onto her nose and pushed away the black cat, who had started to rub against her leg. Then he moved to Ms. Baxter, who sneezed demurely but pointedly; Ms. Widmer scooped him up and took him downstairs.

"The overall goal," said Mrs. Poindexter sonorously, looking over the tops of her spectacles, "is $150,000 for rising expenses like salaries and badly needed new equipment —in the lab, for example—and $150,000 for renovations. We don't actually have to have the cash by the end of the campaign, but we'd like to have pledges for that amount, with their due dates staggered so we can collect $100,000 a year for the next three years. And by next fall, we'd like to have thirty-five new students—twenty in the Lower

School, ten in the freshman class, and five in the sophomore class. So far, we have only four new Lower School prospects and one freshman, and less than half the money has been pledged."

Conn whistled.

"Precisely," said Mrs. Poindexter, who ordinarily did not approve of whistling. She began to read from Mr. Piccolo's report: " 'The day of the independent school is seen by many local businessmen, financiers, and area industrialists as being over. Our fund-raising consultant tells me that, college tuition being what it is, people are increasingly reluctant to spend large sums of money on pre-college schooling, even with the New York public schools being what they are. I see this as influencing both the enrollment problem and the lack of donations, and creating constant resistance to our publicity campaign. There is also a feeling that independent schools can no longer shelter children from the outside world—there was mention by one or two people I spoke to recently of the unfortunate incident two years ago involving the senior girl and the boy she later married . . .' "

That, most of us knew, referred to two seniors Mrs. Poindexter had tried to get expelled, first by council and then by the Board of Trustees, back when I was a sophomore. As Ms. Stevenson, who'd argued on their side, had pointed out, their main crime was that they'd fallen in love too young. But all Mrs. Poindexter had been able to see was the scandal when the girl got pregnant.

" '. . . The point of view,' " Mrs. Poindexter went on reading, " 'has been expressed by prospective Foster donors or parents that although once upon a time parents sent their offspring to independent schools to shield them from the social problems supposedly rampant in public schools, now those problems are equally prevalent in independent schools. This kind of thinking is what our publicity campaign must now counteract.' "

When Mrs. Poindexter stopped reading, I raised my hand, and then remembered I was supposedly presiding, so I put it down. "I have a friend who goes to public school," I said, feeling a little odd referring to Annie that way, "and—well, I think they have more of a drug problem, for instance, than we do, and other problems, too. So I wonder if those parents and people are really right about the problems being equally prevalent. But one thing, though—even though my friend's school is kind of rough, it's a lot more interesting than Foster. What I'm saying is that I wonder if some people might want to send their kids to public schools to sort of broaden them. I think maybe more people think independent schools are snobby than used to."

"We will get nowhere," Mrs. Poindexter said severely, "if our own students do not see the value of a Foster education. Eliza, I am surprised at you!"

"It's not not seeing the value of it," Mary Lou said angrily. "That's not what Liza said at all! I think all she was doing was explaining what some of the people Mr. Piccolo talked to might be thinking. And I bet she's right. I used to go with a guy from public school, and he thought Foster was snobby. And that we were too sheltered."

"Oh, but, Mary Lou, dear," Ms. Baxter fluttered, "neither you nor Liza is very sheltered, though, really—are you? That is, if both of you have been—er—associating with people from other schools, and, as you say, you have been. And that is fine," she added hastily. "Very good, in fact." She glanced anxiously at Mrs. Poindexter. "We must remember," she said gently, "that it takes all kinds. The good Lord made us all."

"I am not sure," said Mrs. Poindexter, "but what this is all entirely beside the point. It is our job to sell Foster's advantages to people—not to imagine disadvantages, or to dwell on the questionable influence students from outside schools may have."

"Questionable influence!" I burst out before I could stop myself, and Mary Lou—she had worn that public-school guy's ring for nearly a year—got very red. Conn shook his head at her and put his hand on my arm, whispering, "Watch it, Liza."

Well, the whole meeting fell apart then—we spent a lot of time arguing instead of deciding what to do. "It's just that in order to combat other people's attitudes we have to understand them first," Conn said after about half an hour more. But Mrs. Poindexter still couldn't see it as anything but unkind criticism of her beloved Foster.

Finally, though, we decided to have a big student rally the Friday after spring vacation, and we planned to try and urge each student either to recruit a new student or to get an adult to pledge money. Walt muttered, "Nickels and dimes—Mr. Piccolo says businesses and rich people and industries are the only good sources of money." But Mrs. Poindexter was so enthusiastic about what we could do if "the whole Foster family pulls together" that somehow she managed to convince most of us we might be able to turn the campaign around. Sally and Walt said they would plan the rally, and Mrs. Poindexter said I should help them, as council president; she told us we should consider ourselves a "committee of three." After a lot of backing and forthing, the three of us agreed to have two meetings the next week, before vacation began, and then a final one during vacation, right before school started again.

Then, just as Mrs. Poindexter seemed to be ready to end the meeting and I was trying to decide whether to call for a motion to adjourn or just wait and see if she'd go back to ignoring my being president again, Ms. Baxter raised her hand and Mrs. Poindexter nodded at her.

"I would just like to remind us all," Ms. Baxter said, waggling one of her handkerchiefs as she nervously pulled it out of her sleeve, "that—and of course we are all aware of it—that it is now more essential than ever that all Foster students, but especially council members, conduct themselves both in private and in public in their usual exemplary fashion. We are more in the public eye than we may realize —why, just last week I was in Tuscan's—Tuscan's, mind you, that enormous department store—and a saleslady asked if I taught at Foster and said wasn't it exciting about the campaign and wasn't Foster a wonderful school." Ms. Baxter smiled and dabbed at her nose with her handkerchief. "How wonderful for us all to be able to assure Foster parents and future Foster parents, by our own example, of Foster's highly moral atmosphere. Even outsiders are beginning to see that we are indeed special—that is one of the exciting things about the campaign—what an inspiring opportunity it gives us all!"

"Well put, Ms. Baxter," said Mrs. Poindexter, beaming at her; Ms. Baxter smiled modestly.

"Now we know why she had Baxter come," Mary Lou whispered to Conn and me.

"I'm sure we would all like to show Ms. Baxter our agreement and thank her for reminding us of our duty," said Mrs. Poindexter, looking around the room.

Ms. Stevenson seemed to be thinking about clearing away the Coke cans. That seemed like a good idea to me, too, so I gave Mrs. Poindexter a perfunctory nod and then started to get up, reaching for the tray. But Ms. Stevenson glared at me and I realized that I was going too far.

Sally said, "Thank you, Ms. Baxter," and started clapping, so the rest of us did, too.

"Thank you," said Ms. Baxter, still with the modest smile, "thank you—but your best thanks will be to continue to show the world—and to help your fellow students show the world also—that Foster students are indeed a cut above. For—we—" she sang suddenly, launching into the most rousing but also the most ridiculous of our school songs, "are—jolly good Fosters, for we are jolly good Fosters . . ."

Of course we all sang along with her.

It was a little sad, because none of us, except Sally and, at least outwardly, Walt, was really very enthusiastic. And there were those two old women, whale and pilot fish, eagle and sparrow, heads back, mouths open wide, eyes shining, singing as if they were both desperately trying to be fifteen years old again.

11

*L*ate that afternoon when I got home from the meeting —trying to tell myself I shouldn't call Annie, because she should rest without interruption for her performance— Chad met me at the door, waving a long envelope that said *Massachusetts Institute of Technology* in the corner, and sure enough, it was an acceptance! It's amazing what hearing that someone wants you to go to their college can do for your ego, but when it's also the only college you really want to go to, and the only one you think can teach you what you have to know in order to be the only thing you want to be—well, it's like being handed a ticket to the rest of your life, or to a big part of it, anyway. I couldn't hold all that in, so I did call Annie after all, and she'd gotten into Berkeley. We decided to go to the Brooklyn Botanic Garden the next day no matter what, to celebrate spring and acceptances and the coming of vacation next week— hers started the same day mine did and lasted as long, be- cause there were going to be special teachers' meetings at her school after the official public-school vacation week. Then, when I got off the phone and went to the dinner table, Dad produced a bottle of champagne, and so it was a very merry Winthrop family who went uptown that night to hear Annie sing.

I don't think it was the champagne I'd drunk that made Annie look so beautiful that night, because I noticed that most people in the audience had dreamy, faraway looks on their faces when she was singing. For me it was as if the concert were hers alone, although three other kids sang and someone played the piano—very well, Mom said. Annie had on a long light blue corduroy skirt that looked like velvet and a creamy long-sleeved blouse, and her hair was down over one shoulder, gleaming so softly under the lights that I found myself clenching my hands at one point because I wanted so much to touch it.

Annie had said that she'd be singing more for me than for anyone else that night, and that there was one song in particular she wanted me to hear. When she began the only Schubert song on the program, she raised her eyes way over the heads of the audience and her special look came over her face, and it was as if she poured everything she was into her voice. Listening to her brought tears to my eyes, though the song was in German and I couldn't understand the words; it made me want to give Annie all of myself, forever.

"Of course that was the one that was for you!" she said the next day in the Botanic Garden when I asked her about the Schubert.

There were hills of daffodils behind us, and clouds of pink blossoms, and the smell of flowers everywhere. Annie sang the Schubert again, in English this time:

"Softly goes my song's entreaty
Through the night to thee.

In the silent woods I wait thee,
Come, my love, to me . . ."

"It's called *Ständchen*," she said when she'd sung it all. "Serenade." And then: "I've missed you so much, Liza, having to spend all that time rehearsing."

Two elderly people came toward us, a woman carrying a canvas tote bag and a man carrying a small camera tripod. Their free hands were linked, and when they'd gone by, so were Annie's and mine.

We walked a lot, hand in hand when there was no one around and once or twice even when there was, because no one seemed to care and the chance of our meeting anyone who would—family, people from our schools—seemed remote. Sometimes Annie told me the names of the flowers we passed and sometimes I made purposely wrong guesses. "Tulip," I said once for daffodil. Annie laughed her wonderful laugh, so I said "Oak?" when we passed a whole bank of little white flowers, and she laughed again, harder.

We ended up in the Japanese Garden, which is just about the prettiest part of the whole place, especially in spring when nearly every tree is blossoming. We sat under a tree on the other side of the lake from the entrance and talked, and caught and gave each other the blossoms that floated down and brushed against us.

We talked a little about Sally, I remember, and how pious she'd gotten, and I told Annie about the special council meeting and how Ms. Baxter and Mrs. Poindexter had sung the school song. And we talked about the recital and how it was the last one Annie would ever be in at her high school. That brought us to a subject we'd been avoiding: graduation and the summer. Annie was going to be a counselor at a music camp in California—I'd known that for a while, but I don't think it really hit either of us till that day that we'd be away from each other from June 24, which was when Annie had to be at the camp, till maybe Christmas, assuming we both came home from college then. Until college acceptances had actually come, college had seemed so far in the future it couldn't touch us, like old age, maybe. But now it was as if, faced with it, we wanted to go back and think it over again—we were being swept along on decisions we'd made before we'd even met each other, and suddenly we didn't feel as triumphant about getting in as we had yesterday when we'd first heard.

We'd been sitting very close together, talking about that, and then we got very silent. After a few minutes, though, we turned toward each other and—I don't know how to explain this, really, but as soon as our eyes met, I knew that I didn't want to be sitting outdoors in public with Annie, having to pretend we were just friends, and I could tell she didn't either, and we both knew that there was no problem now about our not wanting the same thing at the same time, and not much problem about being scared.

"There's no place, is there?" Annie said—at least I think she did. If Annie did speak, I probably answered, "No," but I'm not sure if we actually said the words.

We sat there for quite a while longer, Annie's head on my shoulder, until some people came around to our side of the lake. Then we just sat there, not being able to touch each other.

That night, after Annie and I had spent the rest of the day walking because there was nothing else we could do, I was lying in bed not able to sleep, thinking about her, and —this is embarrassing, but it's important, I think—it was as if something suddenly exploded inside me, as if she were really right there with me. I didn't know then that a person could feel that kind of sexual explosion from just thinking, and it scared me. I got up and walked around my room for a while, trying to calm myself down. I kept wondering if that kind of thing had ever happened to anyone else, and whether it could happen to anyone or just gay people— and then I stopped walking, the thought crashing in on me more than I'd ever let it before: *You're in love with another girl, Liza Winthrop, and you know that means you're probably gay. But you don't know a thing about what that means.*

I went downstairs to Dad's encyclopedia and looked up HOMOSEXUALITY, but that didn't tell me much about any of the things I felt. What struck me most, though, was that, in that whole long article, the word "love" wasn't used even once. That made me mad; it was as if whoever wrote the article didn't know that gay people actually love each other. The encyclopedia writers ought to talk to me, I thought as I went back to bed; I could tell them something about love.

Annie put her arms around me and kissed me when I told her. We were in her room; I'd come for Sunday dinner.

"Encyclopedias are no good," she said, going to her closet and pulling out a battered, obviously secondhand book. *Patience and Sarah*, it said on the cover, by Isabel Miller.

"I've had it for a couple of weeks," said Annie apologetically. "I wanted to give it to you, but—well, I guess I wasn't sure how you'd take it."

"How I'd take it!" I said, hurt. "How'd you think I'd take it? I'm not some kind of ogre, am I?"

"It's just that you still didn't seem sure," said Annie quietly, turning away. "I was going to show it to you sometime—really. Oh, Liza, don't be mad. Please. It's a lovely book. Just read it, okay?"

I did read the book, and Annie reread it, and it helped us discuss the one part of ourselves we'd only talked around so far. We read other books, too, in the next week, trying to pretend we weren't there when we checked them out of the library, and we bought—terrified—a couple of gay magazines and newspapers. I felt as if I were meeting parts of myself in the gay people I read about. Gradually, I began to feel calmer inside, more complete and sure of myself, and I knew from the way Annie looked as we talked, and from what she said, that she did also.

And when on the first day of spring vacation Annie came with me to feed Ms. Stevenson's and Ms. Widmer's cats, we suddenly realized we did have a place to go after all.

12

It started slowly, so slowly I don't think either of us even realized what was happening at first.

I remember Annie's face when we first went into the house. All the delight from her special laugh went into her eyes. I showed her all over the first two floors; it didn't occur to us to go upstairs—somehow that seemed private. Annie loved everything: of course the plants and the gardens outside and the cats most of all, but also the brick-work, the books, the records, the paintings. The cats took to her right away, rubbing against her and purring and letting her pick them up and pat them. She took over the feeding job without our even discussing it.

That first day, I stood in the kitchen leaning against the counter watching Annie feed the cats, and I knew I wanted to be able to do that forever: stand in kitchens watching Annie feed cats. Our kitchens. Our cats. There she was, with her long black hair in one braid down her back, and her blue shirt hanging out around her jeans, and her sneakers with the holes in them and a cat at each one, looking up and mewing.

So I went over and put my arms around her and kissed her, and it became a different kind of kiss from any be-tween us before.

I remember that she still had the cat-food can in her hand and that she nearly dropped it.

After a while, Annie whispered, "Liza, the cats," and we moved away from each other and she fed them. But when she finished, we just stood there looking at each other. My heart was pounding so loud I was sure Annie could hear it. I think it was partly to muffle it that I put my arms around her again. We went up to the living room . . .

I remember so much about that first time with Annie that I am numb with it, and breathless. I can feel Annie's hands touching me again, gently, as if she were afraid I might break; I can feel her softness under my hands—I look down at my hands now and see them slightly curved, feel them become both strong and gentle as I felt them become for the first time then. I can close my eyes and feel every motion of Annie's body and my own—clumsy and hesitant and shy—but that isn't the important part. The important part is the wonder of the closeness and the unbearable ultimate realization that we are two people, not one—and also the wonder of that: that even though we *are* two people, we can be almost like one, and at the same time delight in each other's uniqueness.

. . . *We can be almost like one* . . .

They were wonderful, those two weeks of spring vacation; it was as if we finally had not only a place but a whole world all our own. We even bought instant coffee and food for breakfast and lunch so we could stay at the house all day every day till we both had to go home for dinner. The weather was warm and hopeful, and every morning when I arrived I would fling open the windows and let the sun and the soft spring air pour in. I'd put water on for coffee and then settle down to wait for Annie, sometimes with a newspaper; sometimes I'd just sit there. And pretty soon I'd hear the door latch turning. We had only one key, so I always left the door unlocked in the mornings; Annie could just come in, as if she lived there.

One morning during the first week, I sat at the kitchen counter on one of two tall stools watching the sun give the black cat's fur highlights like those in Annie's hair. Then I heard Annie open the door and come down the stairs to me. I smiled, because I could hear her singing.

"Hi." She kissed me and wriggled out of her lumber jacket, which by then I knew she had gotten secondhand from a cousin. "I got us some more of that Danish," she said, putting a paper bag on the counter.

"But you haven't the money!" I got up and began breaking eggs into a bowl.

"It's all right," she said, giving me a quick hug and then spooning instant coffee into mugs. "Mmm. Coffee smells good, even raw!"

I laughed. "Have some," I said, beating the eggs.

Annie shook her head and opened the refrigerator. "Juice first. I'm starved. I woke up at five-thirty and the sun was so pretty I couldn't go back to sleep. I wanted to come right down here."

"Maybe I should give you the keys," I said, thinking of how wonderful it would be to arrive in the morning and find Annie there waiting for me.

"Wouldn't be right," Annie said. She poured herself

147

some juice—juice makes me feel sick on an empty stomach, and Annie already knew that and never asked me any more if I wanted any. She drank the juice and then scooped up the black cat. "Good morning, puss, where's your brother?"

"Chasing his tail under Ms. Widmer's desk when last seen. Butter, please."

Annie handed me the butter with a bow, saying like an operating-room nurse, "Butter."

I caught her mid-bow and kissed her again, and we stood there forgetting breakfast in the early-morning sun.

We finally did eat, though, and washed the dishes. I remember that morning we were especially silly; it must have been the sun. We had the back door open, and it streamed in through the screen, making both cats restless.

" 'There was an old woman,' " Annie sang, drying a coffee mug, " 'who swallowed a fly . . .' Come on, Liza, you sing, too."

"I can't," I said. "I can't carry a tune."

"Everyone can carry a tune."

"I can't carry one right. I change key."

"Demonstrate."

I shook my head; I've always been self-conscious about singing.

But Annie went ahead with the song anyway, ignoring me, and by the time I was scrubbing the frying pan, I couldn't help but join in. She pretended not to notice.

After we finished the dishes, we took the cats out and watched them chase bugs in the sun on the cobblestones. A heavyset woman in a print housedress and a man's baggy sweater waddled over, peering at us suspiciously. "Katherine and Isabelle," she said with an accent, "I thought they were on vacation? You friends of Benjy's? He usually comes to feed the kitties."

We explained, and she smiled and pulled up her garden chair and sat chatting with us for over an hour. We kept trying to signal each other to do something that would make her go away, but neither of us could think of anything, and she was too nice to be rude to. Finally, though, Annie said, "Well, I'm going in—I've got to do some homework," and the woman nodded and said, "Good girl, never neglect your studies. I should get to the GD vacuuming, myself. If I'd have studied more when I was your age, maybe I'd have gotten myself a good job instead of just a husband and five kids and a stack of dirty dishes."

"She didn't sound as if she really minded," Annie said when we were back inside, up in the living room, Annie with her history reading list and me with my half-finished solar-house floor plan.

We worked, mostly in silence, till lunch—and that day, because it was so warm, we risked meeting the woman again and took our tuna-fish sandwiches out into the back yard. She wasn't there, so Annie went back for the bottle of wine we'd splurged on.

"I'd love to work in that garden," Annie said when we'd finished our sandwiches and were lazily sipping the end of the one glass of wine each we'd allowed ourselves—no one else was outside, still.

"I bet they wouldn't mind."

But Annie shook her head. "I'd mind if I were them," she said. "A garden's special—more than a house. To a gardener." She got up and knelt on the cobblestones, examining the few plants that were beginning to come up around the fading crocuses. The sun was shining on her hair, making little blue-gold strands among the black.

"I'm so lucky," I said.

She turned and smiled at me.

I hadn't even realized I'd spoken till she turned, her head tipped inquisitively to one side, her small round face and her deep eyes intent on me.

"So lucky," I said, holding out my hand.

We went inside.

It was new every time we touched each other, looked at each other, held each other close on the uncomfortable living-room sofa. We were still very shy, and clumsy, and a little scared—but it was as if we had found a whole new country in each other and ourselves and were exploring it slowly together. Often we had to stop and just hold each other—too much beauty can be hard to bear. And sometimes, especially after a while, when the shyness was less but we still didn't know each other or ourselves or what we were doing very well—once in a while, we'd laugh.

The best thing about that vacation was that we somehow felt we had forever and no one could disturb us. Of course that was an illusion, but we were so happy we didn't let that thought touch us.

I'm afraid I didn't think much about the rally or the fund-raising campaign. I had gone to both the meetings the "committee of three" had before vacation, and had reluctantly agreed to write a speech and rehearse it at our last meeting—the one during vacation—and give it at the rally. Nothing I said convinced Sally and Walt that I'd be terrible at it. Walt had gotten a newspaper reporter his older brother knew to say he'd "cover" the rally, which didn't make me any more relaxed about my speech.

"Can't you see it?" Sally had said at our last meeting, I suppose to entice me with dreams of glory. " 'Student Council President Tells What Foster Means to Her— Encourages New Students to Apply.' "

"With one of those smaller headlines underneath," said Walt, "saying 'Save Our School, Cry Students.' Hey, that'd really get 'em, I bet! I wonder if we could get some kids to chant that—spontaneously, of course."

"Don't count your speeches before they're written," I said, trying feebly to be funny. "Or your chants, either."

It's not that I meant to avoid the speech; once it became clear I'd have to make it, I did try to work on it. In fact, Annie and I must have spent nearly all afternoon that first Friday trying to work out what I could say that wouldn't sound phony. And by the time she got through going over it with me, I actually found there were quite a few reasons why I thought Foster was a good school.

But then came the second week, and Annie and I became more comfortable with each other, and the speech and the third meeting slowly slipped far from my mind.

13

It was nearly the end of vacation—Thursday morning of the second week—that I couldn't find the orange cat, so when Annie got to the house, we both hunted in all the places we knew he usually hid. Finally Annie said maybe he'd gone upstairs, and she went up to the third floor to look for him.

It's funny, since we were practically living in the house by then, but neither of us had yet been up there. I think we still felt it was private; that it was okay for us to take over the rest of the house, but not where Ms. Stevenson and Ms. Widmer slept.

After Annie had been upstairs for a few minutes, she called to me in a funny voice. "Liza," she said, sort of low and tense. "Come here."

I went up the narrow stairs and followed her voice into the larger of the two bedrooms. She was standing beside a double bed, the cat in her arms, looking down at the books in a small glass-fronted bookcase.

I looked at them, too.

"Oh, my God," I said then. "They're gay! Ms. Stevenson and Ms. Widmer. They're—they're like us . . ."

"Maybe not," Annie said cautiously. "But . . ."

I opened the glass doors and read off some of the titles:

Female Homosexuality, by Frank S. Caprio. *Sappho Was a Right-On Woman*, by Abbott and Love. *Patience and Sarah*—our old friend—by Isabel Miller. *The Well of Loneliness*, by Radclyffe Hall.

The cat jumped out of Annie's arms and scurried back downstairs to his brother.

"It's funny," Annie said. "I never met them, but from everything you told me, I—well, I wondered."

"It never even crossed my mind," I said, still so astonished I could only stare at the double bed and the books. Certainly at school Ms. Stevenson and Ms. Widmer never gave any hint of being gay—and then it hit me that the only "hints" I could think of were clichés that didn't apply to them, like acting masculine, or not getting along with men, or making teacher's pets of girls. True, once Ms. Stevenson got mad when a kid made a crummy anti-gay remark. But I'd heard my own father do that, just as he did when someone said something anti-black or anti-Hispanic.

Annie picked up one of the books and flipped through it. "Imagine buying all these books," she said. "Remember how scared we were?"

I nodded.

"God, some of these are old," Annie said, turning back to the books in the case. "Ms. Stevenson and Ms. Widmer must go back quite a long time."

Then she closed the bookcase and came over to me, leaning her head on my shoulder. "It's terrible," she said, "for us to have been so scared to be seen with books we have every right to read." She looked up and put her hands on my shoulders; her hands were shaking a little. "Liza, let's not do that. Let's not be scared to buy books, or

153

embarrassed, and when we buy them, let's not hide them in a secret bookcase. It's not honest, it's not right, it's a denial of—of everything we feel for each other. They're older, maybe they had to, but—oh, Liza, I don't want to hide the—the best part of my life, of myself."

I pulled her to me; she was shaking all over. "Annie, Annie." I said, smoothing her hair, trying to soothe her. "Annie, take it easy, love; I don't want to hide either, but . . ."

"The best part," Annie repeated fiercely, moving out of my arms. "Liza—this vacation, it's been—" She went back to the bookcase, thumping her palm against the glass doors. "We can't close ourselves in behind doors the way these books are closed in. But that's what's going to happen as soon as school starts—just afternoons, just weekends—we should be together all the time, we should . . ." She turned to me again, her eyes very dark, but then she smiled, half merry, half bitter. "Liza, I want to run away with you, to elope, dammit."

"I—I know," I said; the bitterness had quickly taken over. I reached for her hands. "I know."

Annie came into my arms again. "Liza, Liza, nothing's sure, but—but I'm as sure as a person can be. I want to hold on to you forever, to be with you forever, I . . ." She smiled wistfully. "I want us to be a couple of passionless old ladies someday together, too," she said, "sitting in rocking chairs, laughing over how we couldn't get enough of each other when we were young, rocking peacefully on somebody's sunny porch . . ."

"On *our* sunny porch," I said. "In Maine."

"Maine?"

"Maine."

We were both calmer now, holding hands, smiling.

"Okay," Annie said. "And we'll rock and rock and rock and remember when we were kids and were taking care of somebody else's house and they turned out to be gay, and how tense we were because we knew we'd have to spend the next four years away from each other at different colleges, not to mention that very summer because I had to go to stupid camp . . ."

We pulled ourselves out of that room, we really did. We went into the other bedroom, because we had to do something and because we were curious, and it was just as we expected; the other bedroom didn't count. All the clothes were in the two closets in the big bedroom and in the two bureaus there, and in the bureau in the other room there were only what looked like extras—heavy sweaters and ski socks and things like that. The bed in that room was a single one and the sheets on it looked as if they'd been there for years. It was just for show.

"We won't do that," Annie said firmly when we were back downstairs in the kitchen, heating some mushroom soup. "We won't, we won't. If people are shocked, let them be."

"Parents," I said, stirring the soup. "My brother."

"Well, they'll just have to know, won't they?"

"You going to go right home and tell Nana you're gay, that we're lovers?" I asked as gently as I could.

"Oh, Liza."

"Well?"

"No, but . . ."

I turned down the gas; the soup was beginning to boil. "Bowls."

Annie reached into the cupboard. "Bowls."

"And if you're not going to run home and tell them now, you probably won't later."

"They won't mind so much when I'm older. When we're older."

I poured the soup into the bowls and opened a box of crackers I had bought the day before. "It won't make any difference. It'll be just as hard then."

"Dammit!" Annie shouted suddenly. "Speak for yourself, can't you?"

My soup bowl wavered in my hand; I nearly dropped it. And I wanted to carry it to the sink and dump the soup down the drain. Instead I poured it back into the pot, reached for my jacket, and said as calmly as I could, "I'm going out. Lock up if you leave before I get back, okay?"

"Liza, I'm sorry," Annie said, not moving. "I'm sorry. It —it's the bed—knowing it's there when the sofa's so awful, and knowing it's going to be so long till we can be together again, really together, I mean. Please don't go. Have your soup—here." She took my bowl to the stove and poured my soup back in it. "Here—please. You're probably right about my parents."

"And you're right," I said, following her into the dining room, "about the bed."

We ate lunch mostly in silence, and afterwards we went up to the living room and listened to music. But Annie sat in an easy chair all afternoon and I sat on the sofa, and we didn't mention the bed again, or go near each other.

156

The next day, Friday, the day before Ms. Widmer and Ms. Stevenson were due home, we cleaned the house and made sure everything was the way we'd found it, and then we went for a long, sad walk. My parents and Chad were going out for dinner that night, and for the first time in my life I was really tempted to lie to them and say I was spending the night at Annie's and ask Annie to tell her parents she was spending the night at our apartment, so we could both spend it in Cobble Hill. But I didn't even mention it to Annie—although I think I lived every possible minute of it in my imagination—until the next morning, when it was too late to arrange for it to happen.

"Oh, Liza," Annie said when I told her. "I wish you'd said. I thought the same thing."

"We'd have done it, wouldn't we?" I said miserably, knowing it would have been wrong of us, but knowing it would have been wonderful, too, to have a whole night with Annie, in a real bedroom—to fall asleep beside her, to wake up with her.

"Yes," she said. Then: "But it wouldn't have been right. It—we shouldn't have been doing any of this. In someone else's house, I mean."

I filled the cats' water dish—we were feeding the cats for the next-to-last time and they were wrapping themselves around Annie's legs, expectantly. "I know. But we did—and I'm not going to regret it. We've put everything back. They don't have to know anything."

But I was wrong about that.

It rained on Saturday, hard. We'd planned to go for another walk after feeding the cats, or to the movies or a museum or something. Without talking about it, we had decided to avoid staying in the house any more. But the rain was incredible, more like a fall rain than a spring one —biting and heavy.

"Let's stay here," Annie said, watching the rain stream darkly past the kitchen window while the cats ate. "Let's just listen to music. Or read. We—we can be—oh, what should I call it? Good isn't the right word. Restrained?"

"I'm not sure I trust us," I think I said.

"It's not wrong, Liza," Annie said firmly. "It's just that it's someone else's house."

"Yeah, I know."

"My Nana should see you now," she said. "You're the gloomy one." She tugged at my arm. "I know. I saw *Le Morte d'Arthur* in the dining room. Come on. I'll read you a knightly tale."

I wonder why it was that so often when Annie and I were tense about the most adult things—wanting desperately to make love, especially in that bedroom as if it were ours—we turned silly, like children. We could have gone out for a walk, rain or no. We could have sat quietly and listened to music, each in our own part of the room, like the day before. We could even have finished leftover homework. But no. Annie read me a chapter out of the big black-and-gold King Arthur, dramatically, with gestures, and I read her one, and then we started acting the tales out instead of reading them. We used saucepans for helmets and umbrellas with erasers taped to the ends for lances, and gloves for gauntlets, and we raced around that house all morning, jousting and rescuing maidens and fighting dragons like a couple of eight-year-olds. Then the era changed;

we abandoned our saucepan helmets and Annie tied her lumber jacket over her shoulders like a *Three Musketeers*-type cape. With the umbrellas for foils, we swashbuckled all over the house, up and down stairs, and ended up on the top floor without really letting ourselves be aware of where we were. I cried "Yield," and pretended to pop Annie a good one with my umbrella, and she fell down on the big bed, laughing and gasping for breath. "I yield!" she cried, pulling me down beside her. "I yield, *monsieur;* I cry you mercy!"

"Mercy be damned!" I said, laughing so hard I was able to go on ignoring where we were. We tussled for a minute, both of us still laughing, but then Annie's hair fell softly around her face, and I couldn't help touching it, and we both very quickly became ourselves again. I did think about where we were then, but only fleetingly; I told myself again that no one would ever have to know.

"You've got long hair even for a musketeer," I think I said.

Annie put her hand behind my head and kissed me, and then we just lay there for a few minutes. Again I wasn't sure which was my pulse, my heartbeat, and which were hers.

"There's no need for us to pretend to be other people any more, ever again, is there, Liza?" Annie said softly.

My eyes stung suddenly, and Annie touched the bottom lids with her finger, asking, "Why tears?"

I kissed her finger. "Because I'm happy," I said. "Because your saying that right now makes me happier than almost anything else could. No—there's no need to pretend."

"As long as we remember that," Annie said, "I think we'll be okay."

"So do I," I said.

It got dark outside early that afternoon, because of the rain, and it was already like twilight in the house. One of us got up and pulled the shade down most of the way, and turned on a light in the hall. It made a wonderful faraway glow and touched Annie's smooth soft skin with gold. After the first few minutes, I think most of the rest of our shyness with each other vanished.

And then, after a very long time, I heard a knock, and downstairs the handle of the front door rattled insistently.

Dear Annie,

It's late as I write this. Outside, it's beginning to snow;
I can see big flakes tumbling lazily down outside my
window. The girl across the hall says December is early
for snow in Cambridge, at least snow that amounts to
anything. January and February are the big snow months,
she says.

"Know the truth," Ms. Widmer used to quote—
remember we used to say it to each other?—"and the truth
will make you free."

Annie, it's so hard to remember the end of our time in
Ms. Stevenson's and Ms. Widmer's house; it's hard even
to think of it. I read somewhere the other day that love
is good as long as it's honest and unselfish and hurts no
one. That people's biological sex doesn't matter when it
comes to love; that there have always been gay people; that
there are even some gay animals and many bisexual ones;
that other societies have accepted and do accept gays—so
maybe our society is backward. My mind believes that,
Annie, and I can accept most of it with my heart, too,
except I keep stumbling on just one statement: as long as it
hurts no one.

Annie, I think that's what made me stop writing to you last June.

Will I write to you now—will I send this letter, I mean? I've started others and thrown them away.

I don't know if I'll mail this. But I think I'll keep it for a little while . . .

14

When the door handle rattled, Annie and I both froze and clung together.

I have never been able to forget the look on Annie's face, but it is the one thing about her that I would like to be able to forget—the fear and horror and pain, where a moment before had been wonder and love and peace.

"It's not either of them," I whispered to Annie, glancing at the clock on the night table. The clock said half past six, and Ms. Stevenson and Ms. Widmer had said they'd be home around eight.

"Maybe if we just stay quiet," Annie whispered, still clinging to me—I could feel her shaking, and I could feel that I was shaking, too.

"Open this door," commanded a loud female voice. "Open it this instant, or I'll call the police."

My legs were made of stone; so were my arms. Somehow I kissed Annie, somehow moved away from her and reached for my clothes.

She sat up, holding the sheet around her. A kitten, I thought, looks like this when it's frightened and trying to be brave at the same time.

"Stay here," I said. "I'm the one who's supposed to be

feeding the cats—it's okay for me to be here." I was pulling on my jeans, trying to button my shirt—there wasn't time to put on anything else.

The door handle rattled again and there was more pounding. "Just a minute," I called as calmly as I could. "I'll be right there."

"Liza, I'm coming too," Annie insisted. "You can't go alone."

"It'll look worse, don't you see, if you're there?" I whispered fiercely, pushing her back, her face breaking my heart. "I'm coming," I called.

Annie reached for my hand and squeezed it hard. "You're right," she said. "But be careful. And—Liza? You were right before, too. I wouldn't have gone home and told my parents."

I tried to smile at her, and then I ran downstairs in my bare feet, trying to make sense out of my hair as I went, and trying not to fall over the saucepan helmets that were still on the floor.

I switched on the light, opened the door a crack, and said, "Yes?" I tried to make it sound casual, but my voice was shaking so much I'm sure I sounded just as terrified as I was.

There on the steps was Ms. Baxter, and behind her, staring at my bare feet and at my not-very-well-buttoned shirt, was Sally.

For a minute I think we all just stared. Then Ms. Baxter steadied herself by holding on to the door frame and cried, "Oh, dear heaven, Liza, are you all right?" And then she barged right in past me, glancing quickly around the two rooms, and then I guess she saw the light in the upstairs hall, which of course neither Annie nor I had been calm enough to think of turning out; Ms. Baxter headed for the stairs.

I ran in front of her without even trying to be polite about it, but she brushed me aside.

It was awful, like some terrible farcical nightmare. As soon as Ms. Baxter reached the stairs, I realized Annie should probably have gotten up after all, and I prayed she'd hide in a closet or something. "You can't go up there!" I yelled, to warn Annie—but then Sally pointed to the head of the stairs and said in a choked voice, "What—who is that?"

I looked up and Annie, white-faced, bare-legged and barefoot in just her lumber jacket, ran past, trying, I realized, to hide in the second bedroom. But it was too late. "Stop!" Ms. Baxter shouted. "Who—who are you? Eliza . . . ?"

"A—a friend of mine," I sputtered. "It's all right, Ms. Baxter. We've—we've been taking care of Ms. Stevenson's and Ms. Widmer's cats this vacation, we . . ."

But Ms. Baxter, her face now set like an avenging angel's, was halfway up the stairs.

"You come down!" I shouted crazily, afraid she might hit Annie in her righteous fury; Annie, realizing she'd been seen, was cowering uncertainly at the head of the stairs. But Ms. Baxter just brushed past her, going into the main bedroom.

Annie came downstairs and stood next to me, slipping her hand into mine. Sally was staring at our hands, I noticed, but I realized that couldn't make any difference now.

We all three stood there, listening to Ms. Baxter stomping around, snooping.

"Dear Lord, dear Lord," we heard her moan as she went from one bedroom into the other.

I looked helplessly at Annie.

Sally was still staring at us. "I—I went over to your house," she said to me finally, like someone in a dream. "I thought you might be sick or something, since you didn't come to the meeting this morning . . ."

"Oh, God," I said. I had completely forgotten about the third committee meeting, the one at which I was supposed to rehearse my speech.

"Chad said you were here," Sally was saying, "but I knocked and rang and yelled . . ."

"We didn't hear you," Annie said unnecessarily.

". . . and when no one came even though it looked as if there was a light on somewhere upstairs and maybe down here too, I got scared it was robbers or that something had happened to you, and I didn't know what to do till I remembered Ms. Baxter lived across the way, so I looked her up on the big directory at the gate and she was home and she said we better check before we called the police, so we both banged on the door and—and—Liza," she said, looking at Annie, "you and she, you were—weren't you?"

"Oh, for Christ's sake, Sally" is what I think I said.

Then Ms. Baxter came downstairs and Sally made everything a whole lot worse by bursting into tears and moaning, "Oh, Liza, Liza, you were my friend, and . . . and you . . ."

"I was afraid for a moment I would find young men up there," Ms. Baxter whispered, actually trembling as she put a maternal arm around Sally, "but what I did find—oh, dear heaven—is far, far worse—though I should have known," she moaned, dabbing at her forehead with her handkerchief. "I should have realized right away." She shook her head sharply, as if ridding it of something unpleasant, and then spoke more firmly. "I almost wish I had found young men," she said. "Sodom and Gomorrah are all around us, Sally." She looked with growing disgust at me. "We must face the truth. There is ugliness and sin and self-indulgence in this house—as I have long feared. And to think," she said, regarding me as if I were a toad, "that the president of student council is a—a . . ."

I was so upset, so hopeless at that point, that I just looked right at her, ignoring Sally, and said, "A lesbian? So the . . ." I stopped myself just in time. "So what?"

It was at that moment that I heard Ms. Stevenson and Ms. Widmer come up the steps, thumping their suitcases down outside the door and wondering loudly but without any alarm yet why there were lights on. Then they realized the door was unlatched, and while we all stood there frozen, Ms. Widmer said, "I think we should get the police, Isabelle," and Ms. Stevenson said, "Nonsense, Liza probably left it open by mistake—maybe she's still here. After all, we're early." Then she called, "Liza?" and Ms. Baxter said, "Oh, you won't want the police, Ms. Stevenson; it's Miranda Baxter," and the two of them came in.

Ms. Stevenson nearly dropped her suitcase, and Ms. Widmer, suddenly very pale, did drop hers.

"Good evening, Ms. Baxter," said Ms. Stevenson coldly, looking around. "Sally—Liza . . ." She looked inquiringly at Annie.

Ms. Baxter sniffed and shepherded Sally toward the door. "Isabelle Stevenson and Katherine Widmer," she said, sounding as if she were trying to be a judge pronouncing sentence—or as if she were trying to be Mrs. Poindexter, whale herself now. "I have long feared that the relationship between you two was—is immoral and unnatural. I will not embarrass us all with specifics, but we are neighbors and it has been clear to me for some time that you are not as distant toward each other at home as you are at school. But naturally I hoped I was wrong—oh, I hoped so very much—and I tried not to notice what—what was before me. And I told myself that as long as what you were didn't affect the students, I could be charitable and hold my peace, that I would not cast the first stone . . ."

Here, as I remember, Ms. Stevenson glanced wryly at Ms. Widmer and said, "Good for you, Miranda, how very thoughtful."

"But now—I come in here and find these two—these two young women practically—*in flagrante delicto*—having been given leave to feed your cats and obviously, given your choice of reading matter—I will not call it literature—having also been given leave to use your home as a—a trysting place, a place in which to . . ." Ms. Baxter took out her handkerchief and dabbed at her forehead; I could see that she was sweating and that maybe she even knew she was saying terrible things but that she felt she had to say them anyway. ". . . place in which to indulge in —in unnatural lusts . . ."

"That," said Ms. Stevenson, eyes snapping, "will do, I think, Miranda."

"Easy, Iza," I think Ms. Widmer said, putting a hand on Ms. Stevenson's arm.

"Look," I said in a voice that immediately sounded much too loud, "I offered to feed their cats. They didn't even ask me to. They don't even know . . ." I realized just in time that it might be a good idea not to use Annie's name. ". . . my friend here. I didn't even know . . ."

"Liza," Ms. Stevenson interrupted—thank God, because I think in my confusion I was starting to say I hadn't known Ms. Stevenson and Ms. Widmer were gay. "Liza, the less said, I think, the better." She didn't say it in a particularly friendly way, and I felt worse than I had when it was just Ms. Baxter and Sally who'd walked in on us.

"All right, Miranda," Ms. Stevenson was saying, her voice taut, like a lion on a leash, "would you mind telling us, very quickly before you leave, just what you were doing here in the first place?"

So Ms. Baxter explained about Sally, who was still staring at me and Annie as if we had at least five heads apiece, like end-of-the-world monsters. "And this poor child," Ms. Baxter whined, nearly choking Sally in her protective hug, "this good, repentant child who has given so much of her time and of herself to Foster's cause these last months —this child who may at times in the past have been misguided and unwise but who is, thank the good dear Lord, normal, with a normal young girl's love for her young man —this child had to be dragged into this—this ugliness, this—this nest of . . ."

"But," I protested angrily, "but it's not ugly, there's nothing . . ."

Ms. Baxter cut me off with her look.

"Oh, my dear," she said to Sally, "you can see now why Liza was unable to be a good enough friend to report you for that unfortunate mistake of yours last fall. Immorality in one way, I fear, leads to immorality in others. It's a lesson we all can learn . . ."

"Oh, for God's sake," snapped Ms. Stevenson, her temper lost at last. "Miranda, I am not going to stand here and let you . . ."

Ms. Widmer quickly opened the front door. "I think it's time for you to go, Miranda," she said quietly. "You, too, Sally."

"Oh, absolutely, Sally goes!" said Ms. Baxter, herding her in front of her. "And if you have a shred of decency left in you, you'll send those two home, too. Liza and her —her *friend*." She smiled thinly. "They are minors, I believe."

I wanted to hit her for the way she said "friend."

"Why don't you go look it up, Miranda?" Ms. Stevenson said through her teeth.

"They are also," said Ms. Widmer, "people—who at the very least have a right to tell their side of the story. To someone who will try to listen."

I glanced at Annie, who was in the corner by the stairs, hugging her lumber jacket around her. It was wool and I remember thinking irrelevantly that it must be scratchy against her skin. But Annie didn't look as if she noticed. She also didn't look as if she felt any more deserving of a friendly listener than I did. The saucepan helmets, I kept thinking, and the bed; how are we going to tell them about the bed?

"I trust you realize," said Ms. Baxter as Ms. Widmer held the door open for her and Sally, "that it is my duty to report this entire incident to Mrs. Poindexter."

"Indeed we do," said Ms. Stevenson coldly.

Then they were gone, and the door was shut, and Ms. Widmer, who had been so collected, swayed a little and leaned against it. Ms. Stevenson put a hand on her shoulder and said, "Steady, Kah, we've lived through worse."

Then she turned to me.

I wanted to touch her, to at least reach out to her—even, for one absurd moment, to throw myself at her feet and moan, "Forgive us—forgive me!" I wanted her to blow up, to yell unreasonably the way she had once in the studio when someone hid an unpopular kid's drawing and then someone else spilled black paint on it by "accident." But she didn't do that. She just looked grimly from me to Annie and back again and said, "Let's start with an introduction, Liza, shall we?"

"Isabelle," said Ms. Widmer, "please. Let's not . . ."

"Katherine," said Ms. Stevenson, "what we have here along with a great many other things is a rather serious betrayal of trust. It doesn't matter how compelling the reason," she said, looking hard at me, "and I think you know now that Ms. Widmer and I can guess exactly how compelling it was—that's still no excuse for the way you and your friend have used this house. No excuse."

"No, Ms. Stevenson," I said miserably. "I know it's not. I—I'm very sorry."

"And I am, too," Annie said, stepping away from the stair-corner. "I—we both are. It was terrible of us, wrong

—it's awful, especially—especially since you're like us—I mean . . ."

She was floundering; I was desperate to help her, but I couldn't think.

"You are not," said Ms. Stevenson, picking up a saucepan, "a bit like us. Even in our worst times, I don't think we would ever, ever have betrayed anyone's trust, not like this—not in a way that would give a—a person like Miranda Baxter license to—to . . ." I saw when she turned away that her fists were clenched, and then, horrified, I realized she was struggling against tears.

Ms. Widmer touched her arm. "Come on, Isabelle," she said with amazing lightness. "At seventeen?" She turned to us. "Why don't you go back up and get dressed—I gather you were upstairs?"

I nodded painfully, and Ms. Stevenson turned the rest of the way away. But Ms. Widmer went on, as gently as before. "Isabelle and I will go down to the kitchen and make some cocoa. Give us—yourselves, too—about fifteen minutes. Then maybe we can all talk about this like rational human beings."

For a second I thought Annie was going to throw her arms around Ms. Widmer. But instead she just took her hand and squeezed it, hard.

Ms. Widmer pushed Annie and me toward the stairs. "Fifteen minutes," she said. "Come along, Iza. Cocoa."

"Cocoa!" I heard Ms. Stevenson exclaim as they went down to the kitchen and we went up to the third floor. "What I need is Scotch, dammit, not cocoa!"

"Well, then, darling, you shall have Scotch," I heard Ms. Widmer say, and then we couldn't hear any more.

15

We had the cocoa, and Ms. Stevenson and Ms. Widmer had drinks, but even though for a minute or two it looked as if we'd be able to talk, that didn't last long.

Ms. Widmer was the first to realize that we never had gotten around to the introduction Ms. Stevenson had requested; when we went down to the kitchen, she put her hand out to Annie and said, "I'm Katherine Widmer, as Liza's probably told you, and that's Isabelle Stevenson."

"H—hi," Annie stammered. "My name is Annie Kenyon. I—I'm a friend of Liza's."

Ms. Widmer smiled wryly and said, "You don't say," and we all laughed.

We laughed again when Annie and I explained, a bit self-consciously, about the saucepan helmets. But after that we all got very stiff, Annie and me hiding behind our cups and Ms. Stevenson and Ms. Widmer hiding behind their glasses. Ms. Widmer and Annie both tried to talk, but Ms. Stevenson just sat there, not exactly glowering but not very friendly either, and I couldn't say a word. Finally after about ten minutes Ms. Widmer said, "Look, I guess we're all too upset to sort this out tonight. Why don't you two go home for now and come back tomorrow, for lunch, maybe, or . . ."

Ms. Stevenson glared at Ms. Widmer, and she went on quickly: "Or after lunch—that would be better. Say around two?"

Annie looked at me and I nodded, and then Ms. Widmer walked us upstairs to the front door.

"We stripped the bed," Annie said shyly, putting on her lumber jacket again. "We could take the sheets to the laundry for you."

"That's all right," said Ms. Widmer, although she looked a little startled. "But thank you."

She smiled, as if she were trying to convey to us that everything would be all right, but I saw that her hand shook as she opened the door, and I hurried Annie out ahead of me.

I walked Annie to the subway, but we were both too upset to talk. Annie gave me a quick hug right before she went through the turnstile. "I love you," she whispered, "Can you hold on to that?"

"I'm trying," I said. I'm not even sure I said I love you back to Annie, although I know I was thinking it, and I know I thought it all that night when I couldn't sleep.

Ms. Stevenson and Ms. Widmer seemed a little calmer the next day, outwardly anyway, but Annie and I were both very nervous.

Ms. Stevenson came to the door in jeans and a paint-spattered shirt over a turtleneck; her hair was tied back, and there was, I was glad to see, a brush in her hand.

"Hi," she said, a little brusquely but smiling, and seeming more relaxed and like herself, at least the self that I knew. She put down the brush. "Come on in. Kah!" she called up the stairs. "It's Liza and Annie."

"Be right there," Ms. Widmer called back, and Ms. Stevenson led us into the living room. The orange cat, who was lying on a neat pile of Sunday papers, jumped into Annie's lap as soon as she sat down; he curled up there, purring.

"He likes you," observed Ms. Stevenson awkwardly, taking off her painty shirt and throwing it into the front room.

"I like him, too," said Annie, stroking the cat.

Then Ms. Widmer came downstairs, in jeans also, and I thought again about their being two comfortable old shoes and wondered if Annie and I would ever be like that.

"Well," said Ms. Widmer, sitting down on the sofa. "I don't suppose any of us really knows how to begin." She smiled. "It's funny, but the first thing that comes into my head to say is how did you sleep last night?"

"Horribly," said Annie, smiling also. "You, too, Liza, right?"

I nodded.

"Well," said Ms. Widmer again, "at least we're all starting out equally exhausted. How about some coffee or tea or something to sustain us?"

Annie and I both said yes, and then, while Ms. Widmer went down to the kitchen, Ms. Stevenson sat there with us for a few painfully silent seconds, and then she went downstairs too.

"Oh, God," Annie said when she'd gone. "This is going to be awful."

The black cat came into the room, tail waving gently, and tried to nudge his brother off Annie's lap. I found a catnip mouse under the coffee table and was just getting it for him when Ms. Stevenson and Ms. Widmer came back upstairs with tea things on a tray and a big plate of cookies that none of us ate.

"What," asked Ms. Stevenson abruptly when we'd each taken a cup of tea, "have you said to your parents?"

"Nothing," we both said at the same time.

"Do your parents know—er—about you?"

We looked at each other. "Not really," I said. "I mean, we haven't told them or anything."

"Once in a while we've gotten yelled at for coming home late or not calling," said Annie, "and Liza's father has said a couple of things about 'exclusive friendships' and things like that, but that's about all."

"They're going to have to know," Ms. Widmer said gently. "At least yours are, Liza. Mrs. Poindexter isn't going to keep quiet about this."

"It was wrong of you to use our house like that," Ms. Stevenson said, putting her cup down. "You know that, I think. But—well, I guess one of the things I remembered last night, with Kah's help"—she looked at Ms. Widmer —"is just how hard it is to be seventeen and in love, especially when you're gay. I was too angry last night to think very clearly, but—well, I think I should tell you that despite all the things I said about trust, Ms. Widmer and I might very well have done the same thing when we were seventeen."

"Especially," said Ms. Widmer, "if we'd had a house at our disposal, which we didn't."

176

Annie's eyes met mine, and then she looked at Ms. Stevenson and Ms. Widmer and said, "You—you mean you've known each other that long?"

"Yes," said Ms. Stevenson, "but that's another story. I'm afraid that right now we have to deal with what's going to happen next." She patted her pockets as if looking for something. Ms. Widmer pointed to a pack of cigarettes lying on the coffee table; Ms. Stevenson reached for them and lit one. "As I see it," she said, "we have two sets of problems. One is the accusation that's going to be made against you two, which really just means you, Liza, since Annie's not at Foster. That's why you'd better decide pretty quickly what to say to your parents. And we also have the accusation that's going to be made against us— against Kah and me."

We went on for another hour or so, talking about it and trying to anticipate what was going to happen and trying also to figure out how best to handle it. I guess it helped; it made us feel a little better, anyway. But it didn't do any actual good.

After we left Cobble Hill, Annie and I went to the Promenade and walked until it was time for Annie to go home.

"I think you should tell your parents, Liza," she said.

"I know," I said uncomfortably. "But how? I mean, what am I going to say? Sally Jarrell and Ms. Baxter caught me and Annie making love at Ms. Widmer's and Ms. Stevenson's house when we were supposed to be taking care of the cats?"

"If you jam your hands any deeper into your pockets,"

said Annie quietly, stepping in front of me and pulling them out, "you won't have any pockets. Look," she said, facing me, "I don't have any right to say anything, because there's no real reason so far for me to tell my parents, and I don't think I'm going to, in spite of what I said before. But . . ."

"Why not?" I interrupted. "Just why not?"

"Because I think it would hurt them," Annie said. "I've thought about it now and I think it would hurt them."

"It'll hurt them to know you love me," I said bitterly, turning my own pain onto her.

"No," Annie said, "it might hurt them to know I'm gay. They like you, Liza, you know that; Nana loves you. And they understand about loving friends. But they wouldn't understand about being gay; it's just not part of their world."

"So you're going to spend your whole life hiding after all, right? Even after saying all that back at the house when we found the books?" I knew I was being rotten, but I couldn't stop myself.

"I don't know about my whole life," said Annie angrily. "I just know about right now. Right now I'm not going to tell them. I don't see why you can't understand that, because you don't seem to be going to tell your parents either."

"But you want me to," I said, trying to keep from shouting—there were other people on the Promenade as usual; an old man glanced at us curiously as he shuffled by. And then I said, the words surprising me and then almost as quickly not surprising me, "Look, maybe I don't want to tell them till I'm really sure. That I'm gay, I mean."

For a moment Annie stared at me. "Maybe that's my reason too," she said. "Maybe I'm not sure either."

We stood there, not moving.

"Liza," said Annie, "the only reason I said I thought you should tell your parents is because all hell's going to break loose at Foster, and someone's going to tell them anyway, so it might as well be you. But it's really none of my business. Especially," she added, "since all of a sudden neither of us is sure." She turned and walked away, fast, toward Clark Street, as if she were heading for the subway.

All I could think of then was that Annie was walking away from me, angry, and that I couldn't bear that. It hit me that I could probably bear anything in the world except her leaving, and I ran after her and put my hand on her shoulder to stop her. "I'm sorry," I said. "Annie— please. I'm sorry. You're my lover, for God's sake; of course it's your business. Everything about me is your business. Annie, I—I love you; it's crazy, but that's the one thing I *am* sure of. Maybe—well, maybe the other, being gay, having that—that label, just takes getting used to, but, Annie, I do love you."

Annie gave me a kind of watery smile and we hugged each other right there on the Promenade. "I'm not used to having a lover yet," I whispered into her hair. "I'm not used to someone else being part of me like this."

"I know," said Annie. "Neither am I." She smiled and pushed me away a little, touching my nose with the end of her finger. "That's the second time in about two seconds you've called me your lover. And the third time in two days. I like it."

"Me, too," I said.

"That must prove something," Annie said.

And then we walked some more, wanting to hold hands but not daring to, in spite of the fact that we'd just hugged each other in full view of what seemed like half of Brooklyn.

We never did decide about my parents, and I realized when I got home that I couldn't tell them with Chad around anyway, or didn't want to, and he was around all evening. By the time we were all going to bed and I could have told them, I'd convinced myself that I might as well wait till the next day, to see what Mrs. Poindexter was actually going to do.

I didn't have very long to wait. As soon as I walked in the front door, Ms. Baxter beckoned to me from her desk in the office.

I tried to face her as if I had nothing to be ashamed of or embarrassed about—but I needn't have bothered, for she didn't even look at me. "Mrs. Poindexter wants to see you," she said grimly into the papers on her desk.

"Thank you," I said.

She didn't say "You're welcome."

I certainly wasn't surprised that Mrs. Poindexter wanted to see me, although I hadn't expected she'd get around to it quite so quickly. I had also expected anger from her, not what I found when I walked into her ugly brown office.

She was wearing black again, but this time without the lace. And she was slumped down in her chair—she usually carried herself so rigidly, sitting or standing, that Chad and I often joked about how she must have swallowed a yardstick as soon as she'd grown three feet tall. But that day her shoulders were hunched and her head was buried in her hands, and she didn't look up when I came in.

I stood there for a minute, not knowing what to do. The only thing that moved in the whole room was the minute hand of the clock on the wall, and that moved so slowly it might just as well have been still.

Finally I said, "Mrs. Poindexter? You wanted to see me?"

Her shoulders gave a little quiver, as if she were sighing from someplace deep inside herself, and at last she looked up.

I was so shocked I sat down without waiting for her to invite me to. Her eyes were red around the edges, as if she'd been crying or not sleeping, and every wrinkle in her wrinkled face was deeper than before, as if someone had gone over each one with a pencil.

"Eliza," she said, very softly, "Eliza, how could you? Your parents—the school! Oh," she moaned, "how *could* you?"

"Mrs.—Poindexter," I stammered stupidly, "I—I didn't mean . . ."

She sighed again, audibly this time, shook her head, and reached for the Kleenex box on her desk so she could blow her nose.

"I don't know where to begin," she said. "I simply do not know where to begin. This school has nurtured you since you were a tiny child—a tiny child—how you can have gone so wrong, how you can be so—so ungrateful— it's beyond me, Eliza, simply beyond me!"

"Ungrateful?" I said, bewildered. "Mrs. Poindexter— I—I'm not ungrateful. Foster's done a lot for me and I—

I've always loved it. I'm not ungrateful. I don't understand what that's got to do with—with anything."

Mrs. Poindexter dropped her head into her hands again and her shoulders shook.

"Mrs. Poindexter, are you all right?"

"No," she said, her head snapping up, "no, of course I'm not all right! How could I be, when Foster is not all right? You—those teachers—just when . . ." She put her hands flat on her desk as if to steady herself, and brought her voice down to its normal register again. "Eliza," she said, "you are seventeen, aren't you?"

I nodded.

"Quite old enough to know right from wrong—indeed, until now, you've shown a reasonable sense of morality, that stupid incident last fall notwithstanding. This may surprise you, but"—here she smiled ruefully—"I have even always felt a begrudging admiration for your stand on the reporting rule. Naturally, in my position, I have not been able to support you in that—and of course I have never been able to agree with your stand, because experience has taught me that most young people are not to be trusted. I have admired your idealism, however. But now you—you . . ."

Oh, God, I thought, *why can't she just yell at me?*

"Eliza," she said, looking out the window, "I met Henry Poindexter, my dear late husband, when I was seventeen. If it had not been for my strong religious upbringing and his, we would have—been weak enough to make a serious mistake within a few months of our meeting. Do you understand what I am talking about?"

I nodded again, surprised, trying not to smile nervously

at the idea of there ever having been anything approaching passion in Mrs. Poindexter—even at the idea of her having been seventeen. Then I realized she couldn't see me, so I said, "Yes."

"So I understand the pull that—sex—can have on young and inexperienced—persons. I do not understand the—the pull of"—she finally turned and looked full at me—"abnormal sex, but I am of course aware of adolescent crushes and of adolescent experimentation as a prelude to normalcy. In your case, had I only known about your unwise and intense out-of-school friendship in time . . ."

I felt my whole body tightening. "Mrs. Poindexter," I said, "it's not . . ."

She cut me off. "Eliza," she said almost gently, "I am going to have to suspend you, pending an expulsion hearing, of course. You know I have the authority to act without student council under extraordinary circumstances, which when you are calmer you will agree these are. I think you will understand that if it weren't for the fundraising campaign we might have been able to handle this more delicately—but if one whisper—one whisper—of this scandal goes outside these walls . . ." Her voice broke and she closed her eyes for a moment; then she pulled herself up and went on. "A public scandal," she said, "would not only mean the end of Foster's campaign, but the end of Foster as well."

She looked at me severely, but I didn't know what to say.

"And of course," she went on, "you must be punished for using someone else's home as a—for using someone else's home in that way, no matter how much—encouragement you may have received from the owners . . ."

"But," I said, horrified, "but Ms. Stevenson and Ms. Widmer didn't . . ."

She ignored me. She closed her eyes again and spoke quickly, as if she were reciting—as if she'd written out the words and memorized them the night before. "You understand," she said mechanically, without even anger showing any more, "that it is impossible for you to continue as president of student council, and that it would be unwise and unhealthy for both you and the other students for you to come back to school until this matter has been resolved. Sally and Walt have requested that you be removed from all participation in the student fund drive . . ."

Words stuck in my throat; anger, tears.

She held up her hand; her eyes were open now. "Therefore, I am asking you to go immediately to your locker and pack up your books and other belongings; you will give the text of your speech to Sally, who will revise it if necessary and deliver it Friday at the rally, which you will under no circumstances attend. There will be a trustees' hearing about your expulsion and about what notations will appear on your record—for, in fairness to the students and teachers at MIT, your—proclivities, if firmly established, which I cannot believe they are in one so young, should be known. In fairness to yourself, too, I daresay, to ensure that you will be encouraged to get professional help. You will be notified of the trustees' hearing; you may attend and speak on your own behalf, and because this is so serious a matter, you may bring an attorney as well as, of course, your parents. The Board of Trustees will at that time make a decision specifically about notifying MIT. Eliza," she said, "this is very much for your own good as well as for Foster's. I do not expect you to see that now, or to see that it is difficult for me to act so firmly. But I have no choice, and someday you may even thank me. I sincerely hope so, not because I want thanks, but because I want to think that you will be—be healed, regain your moral sense, whatever is necessary to set you right again." She reached for her telephone; *oh, God,* I thought, panicking, *I should have told Mom and Dad last night!* "I am now calling your parents, though it pains me to do so. I know it is my duty, and I pray that they can help you. And that you will see it is my intention to be absolutely fair." She began dialing, and said, "You may go," again not looking at me.

Mrs. Baxter glanced up as I came out of Mrs. Poindexter's office and passed by the central office. When she looked down again, I noticed through my numbness that her lips were moving, as if in prayer.

Annie, what does being fair mean? I think they were trying to help me at school; I think even Mrs. Poindexter thought she was helping me, especially by talking about immorality. But what really is immorality? And what does helping someone really mean? Helping them to be like everyone else, or helping them to be themselves?

And doesn't immorality mostly have to do with hurting people—if Sally had pierced people's ears against

185

their will, that would have been immoral, it seems to me,
but doing it the way she did was just plain foolish. Using
Ms. Stevenson's and Ms. Widmer's house without per-
mission—that hurt them and was immoral as well as
sneaky—but—

Liza stood; she crumpled what she'd written so far to
Annie—but then smoothed it out again and hid it under
the blotter on her desk.

But, she thought, looking out again at the wet snow,
what we used the house for—was that immoral, too?

I've been saying yes, so far, because of the hurt it
caused . . .

Before I went home that morning, I went down to the
basement to clean out my locker. Luckily not too many
kids were free first period. Still, there were a couple hanging around down there—including Walt. I tried to avoid
him, but he gave me a kind of obscene grin, as if, even
though he didn't want me in the campaign, he now
counted me as one of the guys; I could almost imagine him
asking me how Annie was in bed. Then, when I thought
a couple of other kids were looking at me funny too, I told
myself I was just being paranoid, that Walt had probably
grinned out of embarrassment only.

But then when I got to my locker and opened it a note
fell out that had obviously been slipped in through the
crack.

"LIZA LESIE," it said.

I didn't get home till halfway through the morning because I'd been walking on the Promenade to put off facing Mom.

As soon as I got in the door, I could see she had been crying. But she was really great to me, there's no question. She tried quickly to put her face back together again, and she put her arms around me right at the door, without saying anything, and held me for a long time. Then she pulled me inside, sat us both down on the sofa, and said, "Honey, honey, it'll be okay. Someday it'll be okay, believe me."

I put my head down in her lap and for a while she just smoothed my hair. But then she put her hand under my chin and gently lifted me up. "Liza," she said, "I know what it's like to have no close friends and then suddenly to have one—it happened to me, too, when I was a little younger than you. Her name was June, and she was so beautiful I had to remind myself not to stare at her sometimes. We loved each other very much, the way you and Annie do—maybe not quite so intensely or quite so—so exclusively, but very much. There was one night . . ." Mom looked away, blushing a little, then said shyly, "There was one night when June and I slept in the same bed. At her house, it was. And we—we kissed each other. And then for a while we pretended one of us was a boy— until it got so—so silly and we got so giggly we stopped. Honey, lots of girls do that kind of thing. Boys, too. Maybe boys more than girls. It doesn't mean anything unless —well, I don't suppose I have to draw any pictures, you're nearly grown up. But—what I think I'm trying to say is that feelings—sexual feelings—can be all mixed up at your age. That's normal. And it's normal to experiment..."

I couldn't help it; I knew I had to leave or blurt out angry words I'd be sorry for later. She was making it impossible, impossible for me to tell the truth. I wasn't sure I wanted to anyway, but how could I even think of it now?

I wrenched myself away from her and ran into the bathroom, where I let the cold water flow till it was nearly ice, and splashed it on my face over and over again. I tried to think; I tried so hard to think—but there was only one word in my mind and that word was "Annie."

When I went back into the living room, Mom was standing at the window looking out at the new leaves on the gingko tree outside the window. "Look," she said, pointing to a small gray bird darting among the branches. "I think she's building a nest." She turned to face me, and put her hands on my shoulders. "Liza," she said, looking into my eyes, "I want you to tell me the truth, not because I want to pry, but because I have to know. This could get very unpleasant—you know that. We can't fight it with lies, honey. Now—have you and Annie—done any more than the usual—experimenting is, I know, a bad word, but I think you know what I mean. Has there been any more than that between you—more than what I told you was between me and June?"

Her eyes were somber; there was fear in them, such fear and such pain, and such love as well, that—I'm not proud of it, I make no excuses—I lied to her.

"No, Mom," I said, trying to look back at her calmly. "No, there hasn't."

The relief on Mom's face was almost physical. I hadn't

188

been aware that she'd looked older when I'd first come in, but now she looked herself again. She even seemed a little cheerful, at least in comparison with before, and she patted my shoulder, saying, "Well, then. Now let's try to talk about what really did happen, and about why Ms. Baxter and Sally misinterpreted whatever it was that they saw . . ."

It was a good thing in a way that Dad came in soon after that, because I couldn't concentrate on Mom's questions. All I could do was say over and over in my mind: *You lied to her. You lied to your own mother for the first time in your life. You lied . . .*

When Dad came in—Mom had called him at the office, I found out later, and he'd come home in a cab, not even waiting for the subway—when Dad came in, his face was gray.

Mom got up from the sofa immediately—I couldn't move—and said, "It's all right, George. Liza isn't sure why Ms. Baxter and Sally got so mixed up, but it was all a terrible mistake. I imagine that both Ms. Baxter and Mrs. Poindexter overreacted, especially Mrs. Poindexter—you know how old she's getting, and the campaign is so . . ."

But I could see right away that Dad wasn't paying any attention to that; he wasn't even hearing it. Mom sat back down on the sofa next to me and Dad looked at me, right at me, with his honest brown eyes and said, "Liza?"— and, oh, God, I said, "Dad—can I get you a drink?"

"No thanks," he said, and he went into the kitchen himself and made drinks for him and Mom.

"Look," Dad said carefully, sitting down in his big chair, "this is hard to say. I don't even know how to begin to approach this, but I—first of all, I want you to know that I'll go along with whatever you decide to do; Liza, I'll support you, whatever's true. You're my daughter—I kept saying that to myself over and over in the cab on the way home: She's my daughter, my . . ."

"George . . ." Mom began, but he ignored her.

"You're my daughter," he said again. "I love you. That's the main thing, Liza, always." He smiled weakly. "Ear piercing and all." His smile faded. "But I have to tell you, Liza—and I've said even less to your mother about this than I've said to you, except when you've been late—that as much as I like your friend Annie and admire her singing voice—fond of her as I am, I haven't been blind to how intense you are about her, how intense you both are . . ."

My stomach felt as if icicles were forming in it.

"George," Mom said again—she had taken only one small sip of her drink; she was holding it as if she'd forgotten it and any moment it would slip out of her hand, unnoticed. "George, adolescent friendships are like that—intense—beautiful." She put her arm around me. "Don't spoil it, don't. This is awful for Liza, for all of us; it must be awful for poor Annie, too. And think of Ms. Stevenson and Ms. Widmer."

"Yes," said my father a little grimly, "think of Ms. Stevenson and Ms. Widmer."

My mother looked surprised; the icicles in my stomach extended slowly to the rest of my body.

"I've always wondered about those two," Dad said. Then he slammed his drink down. "Oh, look," he said, "what difference does it make if a couple of teachers at Foster are lesbians? Those two are damn good teachers and good people, too, as far as I know. Ms. Widmer especially

—look at the poems Chad's written this year, look at how good Liza suddenly got in English. The hell with anything else. I don't care about their private lives, about anyone's, at least I . . ." He picked up his drink again and took a long swallow. "Liza, damn it, I always thought I was— well, okay about things like homosexuality. But now when I find out that my own daughter might be . . ."

"She's not, she told me she and Annie are friends only," Mom insisted.

I wanted to tell Dad then; I wanted to tell him so much I was already forming the words. And if I hadn't already lied to Mom, if we'd been alone then, I think I would have.

"Liza," my father said, "I told you I'd support you and I will. And right now I can see we're all too upset to discuss this very much more, so in a minute or two I'm going to take you and your mother and me out to lunch. But, honey, I know it's not fashionable to say this, but—well, maybe it's just that I love your mother so much and you and Chad so much that I have to say to you I've never thought gay people can be very happy—no children, for one thing, no real family life. Honey, you are probably going to be a damn good architect—but I want you to be happy in other ways, too, as your mother is—to have a husband and children. I know you can do both . . ."

I am happy, I tried to tell him with my eyes. *I'm happy with Annie; she and my work are all I'll ever need; she's happy, too—we both were till this happened . . .*

We had a long, large lunch, trying to be cheerful and talking about everything except what had happened. Then my mother took me shopping, saying we might as well use the time to start buying me clothes for MIT. But really I think she took me so Dad would be the only one there when Chad came home from school.

On the way back to the apartment, Mom and I stopped at the fish store and she bought swordfish, which I love, and she cooked all my favorite things that night, as if it were my birthday. But it was a tense meal anyhow, with Chad speaking only when somebody else talked to him—he wouldn't meet my eyes, even when he and I were talking, which wasn't often.

After dinner I called Sally. I didn't know quite what I was going to say—something like I'm sorry it got to you the way it did. But she hung up on me.

Later that night, when Annie called, I was so worked up that all I could do on the phone with her was cry. So she called back later and talked to Mom, who said yes, I'd be okay, and we'd all get through this and things like that. I imagine it wasn't very reassuring.

The next morning when I woke up, the sun was shining in underneath my window shade, and for a second, just for a second, everything was all right. I'd been dreaming—a wonderful dream about living with Annie—and when I woke up, I think I really expected to see her beside me. But of course she wasn't there. And then everything came crashing in again—Sally's shocked face, Chad's, Mom's, Dad's—and it was as if the air were heavy, pressing down on me and making it hard to breathe. I tried to imagine what it would be like if people always reacted to Annie and me that way—being hurt by us, or pitying us; worrying about us, or feeling threatened—even laughing at us. It didn't make any sense and it was unfair, but it was also awful.

I could hear Mom moving around the apartment, and I didn't want to see her, so I just lay in bed for a while, watching the sun flicker under the shade and trying not to think any more. But then I remembered I still had to give Sally my speech, so I got up and dressed, wanting to get it over with as soon as I could.

Before I even got to Sally—I decided to wait for her outside school—I passed two juniors in front of the main building, and one of them was saying something like, "I'd rather have Ms. Widmer any day than a dried-up old substitute." The other one said, "Yeah. But that one they got to teach art—she's not so bad. I mean, at least she's young."

I didn't hear much more; either I turned it off or they stopped talking. Of course, I told myself, since I'm suspended, Ms. Widmer and Ms. Stevenson will have been suspended, too. If I'm having a hearing, so will they, probably.

Then there was Sally. It's funny, I remember it in outline form, sort of, with Sally and me like shadow figures, facing each other on the steps. I said "Hi," or something equally noncommittal, but Sally just stared at me, so I said, stiffly, "Here's the speech. I'm sorry I forgot it yesterday. I'll help you rewrite it if you want."

It was as if she hadn't heard me. She was still staring at me, shaking her head and ignoring the speech, which I was still holding out to her. "How could you?" she said very softly. "How *could* you—with a *girl*? I just can't believe . . . I mean, think if someone else had found out, someone outside. Walt said it could kill the campaign. People should control themselves if they—if they feel that way. It's—it's so disgusting."

I'd been wanting again to tell her that I was sorry she'd been so upset, but now I was too angry. "It doesn't have anything to do with you, Sally," I heard myself saying. "You don't have to be disgusted."

But she was still shaking her head. "Oh, yes, it does have to do with me," she said. "Everything a person does has an effect on others. Everything. Look at the ear piercing."

I tried to tell her that the two things were different, that piercing ears wasn't the same as loving someone, and that she was making all the wrong connections.

But as I pushed my speech into her hands she said, "Loving! Lusting, you mean. Read your Bible, Liza. Ms. Baxter showed me it's even mentioned there. Read Leviticus, read Romans 1:26."

I don't know what I said then. Maybe I didn't say anything. I'm not sure I was able to think any more.

I do remember, though, that I went home and read Leviticus and Romans, and cried again.

16

One of the worst things that happened in that first week was that Mrs. Poindexter questioned Chad.

After school on Wednesday, Chad didn't speak to me; he seemed to be avoiding me, and I had no idea why. He didn't say much at dinner either, but later, when Mom and Dad were watching TV, he came into my room, shut the door, and without sitting down or really looking at me said that Mrs. Poindexter had called him into her office that morning. He said she'd asked him in not very thinly veiled terms about me and Annie and other girls—whether I had more girlfriends than boyfriends, if he'd ever seen me touching a girl, especially Annie—things like that. And, still without meeting my eyes, he told me he'd said "No" to all the questions about girls and "I don't know" to the ones about boys; in other words, he managed to do his best to save my skin without actually lying.

Neither of us said much after that, but he did finally look at me, scared and hurt and embarrassed and full of questions, and I remember thinking: *This is my little brother in front of me, the kid who's always trusted me,* and I knew I couldn't lie to him the way I had to Mom and Dad.

He said, "Liza, I'll go on saying the same things to Poindexter, but I saw you and Annie holding hands once, and you sure spent a lot of time with her at Ms. Stevenson's and Ms. Widmer's house. Is it true?" So I said, "Yes," and then I tried to explain. After I finished, he was quiet a long time again, and then he asked, "Do you think you have to be like that?" Then it was my turn to be quiet, but after a minute I said, "I think I *am* like that." Chad nodded sadly, but not in any kind of disparaging way, and then he hugged me and left.

Later that night, I heard him crying in his room.

And then there was Annie—the hurt I'd seen on her face. She never talked about it. I remember she cut school and came down to Brooklyn the afternoon of the day I saw Sally on the steps, not even calling first, because she was afraid I'd tell her not to come. Mom had gone to the store, and when I answered the door and saw Annie standing there, all I could do was cling to her, especially as soon as I saw her eyes and realized that the hurt was still there. I didn't want to think about what it had done to her to have Ms. Baxter barrel up the stairs and find her the way she had, to have Sally and Ms. Baxter stand there looking at her as if they thought she was a whore.

"Liza, Liza," she said, stroking my hair, "are you okay?"

"I think so," I said. "Annie, are you?"

"No one knows for sure that I'm gay except you and Ms. Stevenson and Ms. Widmer," she said softly, touching my face. "I don't even count Sally and Ms. Baxter. Nobody's doing anything to me. Maybe I *should* tell my parents—I just wish I could share this with you."

"I'm glad you can't," I said. "And I'm glad you haven't told your parents."

"Liza—don't let it make any difference. It won't, will it? With us, I mean?"

"Of course it won't," I told her.

But I was wrong. Six months of not writing—that's a difference.

And so I lied to Annie. On top of everything else, I lied to Annie, too.

Friday afternoon, just about the time when the rally was supposed to be held at Foster, Mom practically dragged me out of the house to the Brooklyn Museum. I couldn't tell you a thing we saw. It wasn't so much that I cared about the rally any more; I didn't, at least not very much. But I did care about my speech. Even though I'd have been nervous giving it, I'd worked on it with Annie, and so it was partly hers.

"The speech was okay, Liza," Chad said when Mom and I got home at about six-thirty. "Sally wasn't as good as you'd have been, but it was okay. Two newspaper people were there, and one of them said he thought it was a good speech. Should raise a lot of money, he told Mrs. Poindexter. I don't think Sally changed it much, either."

After I'd thanked him, I ran into my room and slammed the door.

Saturday I got a letter from Mrs. Poindexter telling me the trustees' hearing would be the following Tuesday evening, April 27.

Sometimes I think the trustees' hearing was worse than when Ms. Baxter barged in; sometimes I'm not sure.

The Parlor looked different that Tuesday night with the trustees in it—maybe because it was night. The hearing had to be then because most of the trustees had jobs during the day.

The only people there I already knew were Mrs. Poindexter, Ms. Baxter, and of course Ms. Stevenson and Ms. Widmer. They had a lawyer with them, a tallish woman in a gray dress with a bird pin on the collar. I don't know why I noticed that pin, but I kept staring at it almost the whole time we—my parents and I—were waiting to go in.

My parents didn't bring a lawyer. I think they were embarrassed to. Mom said she didn't think we needed one, because after all I hadn't done anything, had I? Dad just looked away when she said that. After the hearing, he said he'd get a lawyer if the trustees actually expelled me or decided to put anything on my record.

I wanted to go over and talk to Ms. Stevenson and Ms. Widmer while we were all waiting to go in, but Dad wouldn't let me. He apologized, but he said it wouldn't be a good idea. Both he and Mom smiled at Ms. Stevenson and Ms. Widmer, though, and then we all hung around stiffly in the hall, waiting. Ms. Stevenson and Ms. Widmer and their lawyer were sitting on the wooden settle. Mrs. Poindexter and Ms. Baxter were already inside.

The whole thing felt the way being caught in quicksand must feel, when you know you're not going to be able to get out, especially if you struggle. I also felt as if I were watching my own dream. I was there at the hearing, but I also wasn't there; I said things, I heard what other people said, but as if from a great distance. The only thing that seemed truly real to me was the one thought that wouldn't let go in my mind: *It's Annie and me they're all sitting around here like cardboard people judging; it's Annie and me. And what we did that they think is wrong, when you pare it all down, was fall in love.*

"Steady," my father said, walking into the Parlor between my mother and me when we were called. Ms. Stevenson and Ms. Widmer started to follow us, but the woman who'd called my parents and me waved them back to their seats.

I must have looked pretty meek, walking in there with my parents; I know I was more scared than I'd ever been in my life. Mom had made me wear a dress, and had tried to get my hair to stay in place by making me use conditioner, which I'd never done before, so I didn't even smell like myself, at least my hair didn't. Ms. Stevenson and Ms. Widmer were wearing dresses, too, but at least they did most of the time—skirts, anyway. But it did occur to me that it was as if all three of us were trying to say, "See—we're women. We wear dresses." Oh, God, how ridiculous!

As I walked in, I touched Annie's ring for luck, and tried to remember the words to "Invictus." The first person I noticed was Ms. Baxter. She was sitting there looking very solemn and proper and righteous, as if she'd just been canonized. She was near the end of one side of the same long table that everyone had sat around at the student council hearing. The trustees sat along both sides of the table, also looking very solemn but not quite so holy, and there was an empty chair for me opposite Ms. Baxter, and chairs for Mom and Dad behind mine. I remembered

Sally whispering last fall in the same room, "It's like court on TV," and this time it was even more like that. "The Inquisition," Annie called it later.

Mrs. Poindexter, with a yellow note pad, was sitting under Letitia Foster's portrait, at the head of the table. Ms. Baxter was sitting next to her but on the side, at right angles to her. At the other end of the table, opposite Mrs. Poindexter, was a fat, silver-haired man with tight-fitting glasses that sort of sank into his face. His name, he told me, was Mr. Turner, and he was the head of the Board of Trustees. I know there was a Miss Foster, who was a distant relative of Letitia's. Miss Foster was very old and didn't say anything; I'm not sure she could even hear. There was a woman with reddish hair and a pale face—the youngest of them, I guess, even though she looked middle-aged. She was the only one who smiled at me when I walked in. Next to her was a man in a green corduroy sports jacket and a turtleneck. There were one or two others, but they faded into a blur.

Then it began.

Mr. Turner asked Ms. Baxter to tell in her own words what she'd seen, and told me to listen carefully. She said something like, "Yes, of course, but—oh, dear—you do understand how difficult it is to talk about such things," and the red-haired woman said, sort of dryly, "As I remember, you were the one who lodged the original complaint with Mrs. Poindexter," which made me like her right away. Then, while Mrs. Poindexter put on her glasses and looked down at her notes, Ms. Baxter—Ms. Baxter with the lace handkerchiefs, Ms. Baxter who always went around saying one should believe the best of everyone, Ms. Baxter who said it takes all kinds and the Lord made us all—Ms. Baxter gave this incredibly lurid account of what she'd seen. It was awful. It made us sound like monsters, not like two people in love. That was the worst thing, another thing I'm never going to be able to forget even though I want to. It was as if everyone were assuming that love had nothing to do with any of this, that it was just "an indulgence of carnal appetites"—I think Ms. Baxter actually used those words.

Ms. Baxter also said I was "half-naked" when I came to the door, and that Annie had "scurried guiltily" out of the bedroom, "wearing nothing but a red-and-black shirt"— her lumber jacket, which, of course, was as big on her as a coat.

"What else did you see?" Mr. Turner asked; Mrs. Poindexter smiled at Ms. Baxter over the tops of her glasses.

"Well," said Ms. Baxter, "of course I felt I had to conduct a search, because of my long-standing suspicions about the two older women. It saddened me to do it—but of course I had no choice. I had no idea but what there might be other—young persons of—of similar persuasion somewhere—so I went upstairs. I must say the place was a shambles."

The "shambles," I realized, was because of the umbrellas and saucepans. And part of me wanted to laugh at that absurd line—"persons of similar persuasion"; it sounded like the equally absurd "persons of the Jewish persuasion": "I am of the lesbian persuasion." But it wasn't funny. Even later, when I tried to tell Annie about it, it wasn't.

"Ms. Baxter, please confine your remarks to what you saw involving the two *young* women only," Mr. Turner said, which I thought was pretty fair.

Mrs. Poindexter leaned over and whispered to Ms. Baxter, pointing to something on her note pad. Ms. Baxter stumbled a bit as she said, "Well, they—Liza, when she answered the door—seemed very flustered. She was clutching her shirt closed across her—her bosom, and it was clear she had nothing on underneath, and she was blushing. Then later she kept looking at the other girl—what was her name?"

Mrs. Poindexter took her glasses off and looked right at me, and suddenly there wasn't a drop of saliva in my mouth. I'd already made a promise to myself not to mention Annie's name, on the grounds that the Board of Trustees had nothing to do with her, and Mom and Dad had both agreed with me. Dad leaned forward, but the red-haired woman said quickly, "The other girl doesn't concern us, since she's not a Foster student."

"Well," said Ms. Baxter, "she kept looking at her, Liza did, and poor little Sally Jarrell said something like, 'Oh, my God,' for which I certainly do not blame her—I mean, what a terrible shock it must have been, especially since she and Liza are friends and since Sally is already deeply and maturely involved with a young man . . ."

"Ms. Baxter," said Mr. Turner tiredly, "please confine yourself to what actually happened, not what you thought about it, or thought someone else thought about it."

Ms. Baxter looked hurt. "Eliza ran to the stairs," she said, whining a little now, "and forcibly tried to keep me from going farther, which of course made me certain something else was going on."

I almost leapt out of my chair, but Dad put his hand on my shoulder. "You'll get your turn, Liza," he whispered. "Stay loose."

Ms. Baxter went on. "But since of course I felt it was my duty to—to expose those women once and for all for what they are—of course at that point I only suspected—I went on and—and, well, the rest does have more to do with the women than with the girls, though how one can call people like that women, I'm sure I don't know."

Ms. Baxter sat back, not smiling, but piously, as if she felt sure no one could possibly disagree with her. Mr. Turner looked disgusted, though, and the red-haired woman looked as if Ms. Baxter was something she'd like to squash under her heel. Mrs. Poindexter was smiling nastily. "I would like to add," she said, "that I am grateful to Ms. Baxter for having the courage to bring this entire appalling matter to my attention. I of course did not hesitate . . ."

The man in the corduroy jacket leaned forward, his pencil poised over a yellow pad. "Ms. Baxter," he said, ignoring Mrs. Poindexter, "am I right in deducing that you were far more concerned all along about the women than about the girls? About confirming your"—he consulted his pad—"your 'long-standing suspicions' about the two teachers?"

Mr. Turner looked a little uncomfortable, but he didn't say anything.

"I told you," said Ms. Baxter, "that I have been disturbed for years by my feeling that all is not as it should be between those women, that there is a—a sad, unnatural relationship between them. If two young girls, one of them a Foster girl, were—well, being immoral . . ." Here I almost jumped up again. ". . . in their house, and if I actually saw one of them running half-naked out of the bedroom, I could only assume that there were perhaps more young people, perhaps Foster students, also using the house lewdly, with, I had to believe, Ms. Stevenson's and Ms. Widmer's sanction. I felt it my duty to clarify that point."

Mrs. Poindexter nodded emphatically.

The red-haired woman muttered something sardonically that sounded like "A very orgy," but I'm not absolutely sure that's what she said.

"And when I did go upstairs," said Ms. Baxter, "I found the—er—the bed unquestionably mussed, and I did at the same time just happen to see the books I mentioned in the—er—complaint—horrible obscene books . . ."

"Ms. Baxter," said the red-haired woman, "did you actually see the two girls touch each other in a sexual way?"

"Well," said Ms. Baxter, "they stood there holding hands while I was . . ."

"I said in a sexual way. In an overtly, unmistakably sexual way. Holding hands, especially under stress, doesn't seem to me to be particularly significant."

"Well," said Ms. Baxter, glancing uncomfortably at Mrs. Poindexter, "well, in—er—that kind of way, overtly, perhaps not, but after all, it was plain as day what they had been up to. As I said, the bed was rumpled, and there were . . ."

"I see," said the red-haired woman. "Thank you."

"Any more questions for Ms. Baxter?" asked Mr. Turner, looking around at the members of the board.

"I would just like to remind the board," said Mrs. Poindexter huffily—she had not once looked at me or my parents—"that Ms. Baxter has been in the employ of this school for ten years, and that her record is impeccable."

"Ms. Stevenson and Ms. Widmer have both been at the school for fifteen years, am I right?" asked the red-haired woman.

"Ms. Stevenson and Ms. Widmer," said Mrs. Poindexter, "especially Ms. Stevenson, have become increasingly permissive as the years have passed. In fact, Ms. Stevenson . . ."

"Please," said Mr. Turner, "we are not discussing the teachers now." Then he turned to me, and I guess the twitch at the corners of his mouth was his attempt at a reassuring smile.

"Eliza," he said—and I felt my stomach almost drop out. *"Unconquerable soul,"* I tried to say to myself; *"bloody but unbowed,"* and I touched Annie's ring again and took a deep breath to make myself calmer—but none of it really helped. "Liza, rather. Thank you for coming. I know this is going to be difficult for you, and quite possibly embarrassing. I have to tell you, however, that we would prefer that you speak instead of your parents—of course they may assist you—and if at any time the three of you feel you cannot proceed without counsel, we will adjourn until you can obtain same."

I was a little confused, mostly because of being so nervous, and I guess Dad must have sensed it because he moved his chair next to mine and said, "May I explain to my daughter, sir, that what you mean is that if she wants a lawyer, or we do, the hearing can be stopped until we get one?"

Mr. Turner did smile then, and said, "Certainly, Mr. Winthrop, and I thank you for doing so with such economy. I shall try to use—er—plainer language."

Of course then I felt like a dummy, which didn't help at all.

"Liza," said the red-haired woman, "mostly we'd just like your version of what happened when Ms. Baxter knocked at the door. Can you tell us?"

I didn't know what to say at first, so I licked my lips and cleared my throat and did all the things people do when they're stalling for time. I didn't want to lie any more, but I didn't want to tell them everything either. But finally I realized she hadn't asked me about what had happened *before* Ms. Baxter arrived, so I relaxed a little.

I told them that it had been more or less the way Ms. Baxter had said, except that she'd started to go upstairs before she'd seen Annie and that I didn't think I had "forcibly prevented" her from doing that, although I had tried to stop her. But the more I talked the more I realized it was obvious that I was leaving a lot out—and I also felt more and more that whatever I said wasn't going to make much difference anyway. It was what we were that Mrs. Poindexter and Ms. Baxter were against, as much as what we'd done. As soon as I realized that, I thought it was all over.

"Liza," Mr. Turner said delicately, "Ms. Baxter mentioned that you seemed—er—not quite dressed. Is that so?"

"Well," I began; I could feel my face getting red. "Yes, sort of. But . . ."

206

"What were you wearing, hon?" the red-haired woman asked.

"A shirt and jeans," I said.

"As Ms. Baxter pointed out," said Mrs. Poindexter, "that was obviously all she was wearing."

"Mrs. Poindexter," said Mr. Turner angrily, "this young woman let Ms. Baxter speak without interruption. I think the least all of us can do is extend her the same courtesy."

Mrs. Poindexter grunted. But unfortunately she'd made her point, and I could see the pencils scribbling.

"And your friend?" asked the red-haired woman. "What was she wearing?"

"A—a lumber jacket," I stammered.

"Is that all?" asked the man in corduroy. He sounded surprised.

I felt my throat tighten and I looked desperately around at my mother, who I think tried to smile at me. But, oh, God, that was worse; it was horrible, looking at her and seeing the pain on her face—seeing also that she was trying to be brave for my sake.

I couldn't speak, so I nodded. I could feel my father squirm in his chair next to me, and I thought then that he must at that moment have realized I'd lied to him even if Mom hadn't realized it, or wouldn't let herself.

Mrs. Poindexter got up, walked to the other end of the table, and said something to Mr. Turner. He shook his head and she said something else. Then the whole group of them, except Ms. Baxter, who stayed put, started whispering. My mother glared at Ms. Baxter, and my father reached out and took my hand. "Steady on," he whispered, even though I knew what he must be thinking and feeling. "Just remember that whatever happens it's not going to be the end of the world." But then he and my mother looked at each other and I could see that they pretty much thought it was.

"Liza," said Mr. Turner softly, "I'm afraid I'm going to have to ask you why you and your friend were—er—partly undressed."

At this point my usually quiet mother jumped to her feet and said, "Oh, for Lord's sake! My daughter has already told her father and me that there was nothing untoward going on! Liza is an honest girl, a painfully honest girl. She has never lied to us in her life. Don't you know how teenaged girls are? They're always washing each other's hair and trying on each other's clothes—things like that. There could be a million reasons why they weren't quite dressed, a million reasons . . ."

"Teenaged girls," shouted Mrs. Poindexter, moving around to our side of the table and walking toward my mother, "do not usually try on lumber jackets. And I've never felt that your Liza had any particular interest in her hair. As a matter of fact, I have often felt that your daughter Eliza . . ."

"Yes?" shouted my mother. She looked about ready to swing at Mrs. Poindexter. Dad reached out and grabbed her arm, but she ignored him.

"Ladies, ladies!" said Mr. Turner, standing up. "That will do! I realize how emotionally charged this is—I warned you, Mrs. Poindexter, what might happen if we handled this matter in this way. In any case, we absolutely cannot tolerate this kind of behavior from anyone."

Everyone sat down again, fuming, Mrs. Poindexter included, and I was still left with the question.

"Liza," said Mrs. Poindexter a little sulkily, "answer the question. Why were you and that other girl so incompletely dressed?"

I looked at Dad and then at Mr. Turner. I don't know where it came from, but I said, "I guess this is where I say that I don't want to answer without a lawyer."

"May I point out," said Mrs. Poindexter coldly, "that that statement in itself can be interpreted as an admission of guilt?"

Mr. Turner cleared his throat angrily, but before he could say anything, the red-haired woman threw her pencil down. "I think this is all perfectly absurd," she said. "Not to mention very, very cruel, and downright twisted! What this young woman does on her own time with her own friends is her business and her parents' business, not ours. I must say I might be concerned if I were her parents, but as a trustee of this school, I have more serious things to worry about." She looked at Mrs. Poindexter and her voice dropped a little. "Frankly, Mrs. Poindexter, this— this near-vendetta reminds me of another incident a few years back, the one involving the boy and girl in the senior class. You will all recall it, I'm sure. Perhaps there was some small point in the school's involvement in that, since, because of the girl's condition, the students would naturally become aware of the situation—but I see no chance of that here, or of this incident's getting to the public as you seem to fear it might, and damaging the fund-raising campaign. In fact, I see much more danger of its being publicized as a result of this ridiculously anachronistic hearing than because of the incident itself. The overriding point," she said, looking around at the board members and then at Ms. Baxter and Mrs. Poindexter, "fund-raising campaign or no fund-raising campaign, is whether Liza's conduct affected the other students adversely, or whether something wrong was done on school time or on school grounds. Obviously, the latter doesn't apply, and as to the former—it is certainly unfortunate that Sally Jarrell may have been exposed to something that disturbed her, but she is no more a child than Liza is, and it's clear to me that Liza did not willingly make Sally a party to her behavior. Most people nowadays are fairly enlightened about homosexuality and there certainly was no purposeful wrong here, no attempt to . . ."

"There are the teachers," said Mrs. Poindexter softly. "There is the question of influence—the decided influence that teachers have over students . . ."

"That is a separate issue," said the red-haired woman angrily, "and obviously one of much greater relevance."

Mr. Turner said, "I think we should ascertain if Liza wishes to say anything further to us, and then, bearing in mind that she has requested counsel and that her presence here is voluntary, move to the matter of the two teachers. We can call Liza at a future date, I am sure, if need be, assuming she is willing to be questioned further."

Mrs. Poindexter's lips tightened, and she twisted her glasses chain angrily.

"I agree," said the red-haired woman, "and I apologize for my outburst, Mr. Turner, but this has all seemed to me so—so terribly unnecessary that I couldn't help speaking out. I simply don't see that what the two girls did or didn't do is of any importance whatsoever. What matters is the influence the teachers may or may not have had on them, and on other Foster students."

I think I must have been staring at her, because I remember she gave me a sort of embarrassed and apologetic smile. *It is important!* I wanted to shout; it was as if she'd suddenly betrayed me—the one person on the board I'd really trusted and who I thought had understood. I knew she was trying to be fair to everyone, not just to me, but, oh, God, I wanted to stand up and shout: *No one had any influence on us! Ms. Stevenson and Ms. Widmer had nothing to do with it. What we did, we did on our own; we love each other! Can't anyone understand that? Please —can't someone? We love each other—just us—by ourselves.*

But although most of those words were in my mind by the time Mr. Turner looked at me again and said, "Liza, is there anything else you would like to say?" all I could do was shake my head and whisper, "No, sir."

And much, much later, I thought of what Annie had said about mountains, and felt as if I still had a whole range of them left to climb.

17

$\mathcal{J}$ remember very little about the next few days. I know I saw Annie only twice, and both times we were stiff and silent with each other, as if all the fears, all the barriers, were back between us.

The long thin white envelope came on Saturday when Chad and I were home watching a Mets game. Chad went down for the mail during a commercial. I was sitting there, idly wondering if they were ever going to rewrite the stupid beer ad I was suffering through for the millionth time, when I heard his key scraping in the lock and then his voice saying, "Liza, I think it's come."

He handed me the envelope—from Foster—and I swear he was more scared than I was. He hadn't said much about what it had been like at school for the past couple of weeks while I hadn't been there, but I got the impression it hadn't been any picnic for him. Sally, he'd mentioned casually, wouldn't speak to him. Even though she was a senior and he was only a sophomore, they'd always been friendly enough to say hi in the halls and things like that. Sweet wonderful Chad! One afternoon he came home late with a bloody nose and blood in his sheepdog hair. He ran straight to Dad; he wouldn't speak to me. Neither he nor

Dad ever told me what happened, but I'm pretty sure I know, and it still makes me sick, thinking about it.

"Aren't you going to open it? You want me to go away? I'll go back to the game," he said, and turned toward the TV set.

It's funny, but I didn't feel much of anything, staring at that envelope before I opened it. Maybe it was because by then I really didn't want to go back to Foster anyway, even if they said I could—and so in a way I was dreading not being expelled as much as being expelled. The only thing I was conscious of worrying about was MIT, and whether the trustees would notify them if they expelled me and what reason they'd give.

There was a roar from the TV set—the Mets had just gotten a run. Chad didn't roar, though, and you can usually hear his shouts halfway down the hall outside our apartment.

I stuck my finger under the flap of the envelope and it opened so easily I hoped it hadn't come unglued on the way and that the letter hadn't fallen out in front of everyone in the post office.

Dear Ms. Winthrop,
    The Board of Trustees of Foster Academy is happy to inform you . . .

"Chad," I said. "It's okay."

Chad threw his arms around me and shouted "Hooray!" Then he stepped back, and I must have looked pale or something because he sort of eased me down into Dad's chair and said, "Hey, Liza, you want some water or an aspirin or something?"

I shook my head, but he got me some water anyway, and after I'd drunk some of it, he said, "Aren't you going to read the rest of the letter?"

"You read it," I said.

"Sure?"

I nodded.

So Chad read out loud:

"Dear Ms. Winthrop,

"The Board of Trustees of Foster Academy is happy to inform you that, after due deliberation relative to the disciplinary hearing held on April 27 of this year, we have found no cause for action of any kind in your case, disciplinary or otherwise.

"Mrs. Poindexter has agreed that you will continue in your position of Student Council President. No account of the hearing will appear on your record and none will be sent to any college to which you have applied or at which you have been accepted.

"With all good wishes for the future,

Sincerely,

John Turner, Chairman"

"There's a separate little slip, too," Chad said, holding it up, "saying you can go back to school on Monday."

"I can't wait," I said dryly.

"Lize?"

"Umm."

He looked very puzzled. "Liza—does it mean—you know. Does it mean you aren't—weren't . . . ? But I thought—you know."

"Oh, God, Chad," was all I said, all I could say. And then I went out of the room to call Annie, leaving my poor little brother even more bewildered than before.

After I called Annie, I tried several times to call Ms. Stevenson and Ms. Widmer but wasn't able to reach them. I tried again on Sunday and Annie and I even talked about walking over there, but Annie pointed out that it might be more sensible not to let anyone, especially Ms. Baxter, see us there at least until everything had died down a bit.

Monday was the first really hot day we'd had, almost like summer, but I knew that wasn't why I was sweating by the time Chad and I arrived at school. I wanted to walk in confidently, looking as if nothing had happened, but as we went up the steps, I knew I wouldn't be able to do it.

"If you want us to go in separately, it's okay with me," I told him.

"Are you crazy?" he said. And then he actually held the door open for me, and stared hard at a couple of sophomores who sort of snickered.

"Good luck, Sis," he whispered. "Yell if you need me. I've got a left jab that packs quite a wallop."

I suppose I embarrassed him by doing it, but I hugged him right there in the hall.

Foster felt like a place I'd never been before when I walked through the hall that day and downstairs to my locker. I guess it was mostly that I didn't feel I could trust people there any more, and somehow that made even the familiar shabby walls look potentially hostile.

There were the same rooms, the same people, the same

staircases, the same dark wood and stuffy smell, the same dining room with little vases of violets from the school garden on each table, the same bulletin board on which Sally had put her ear-piercing sign a hundred years ago, my same old battered locker . . .

Would there be another note?

There wasn't.

A couple of kids came to their lockers when I was putting stuff back into mine, and I said hi and they said hi back, but of course it was a little stiff and embarrassed on both sides. Valerie Crabb, who was in my physics class, tried, though. She held out her hand to me and said, "Welcome back, Liza. You want any help making up stuff in physics, say the word." That was really nice.

But then I went into the girls' room and that wasn't so nice. No one said anything specific—but one kid said hi loudly, like a warning: "Hi, *LIZA!*"—and she and another girl who'd been combing their hair left immediately and someone who'd just gone into a booth flushed right away and hurried out without even washing her hands or looking at me.

I told myself it would be great to have the john to myself every time I wanted to use it, but I didn't convince myself.

Then, on the way to chemistry, I ran into Walt.

He stopped right in the middle of the hall when I was still a few feet away and held out his hand to me. "Liza, hello," he said, all smiles. "Hey, it's really good to see you back. I mean that—really good."

I tried to shift my books around so I could shake his hand, since he was holding it out so persistently. "Hi,

Walt," I said, and started walking again as soon as the handshake was over.

He fell into step beside me. "Hey, listen, Liza," he said. "I hope you're not going to let any of this—well, you know —affect you at all. I mean, well, sure Sally was upset, but I want you to know I'm behind you all the way—I can understand Sally's reaction, but—well, I'm not going to desert a friend just because of a little—sex problem or anything. I mean, the way I figure it, it's just like any other handicap . . ."

Luckily we'd just about reached the lab by then, and luckily Walt's first period class was Latin, not chem.

I didn't really notice in chemistry that the only people sitting near me were boys, especially since, when we broke to do an experiment, my lab partner, who was a very intense, brilliant girl named Zelda who was going to be a doctor and who hardly ever smiled, began asking me questions. She started innocently enough, saying, "Welcome back, Liza. I mean that sincerely."

I thanked her, trying not to make as big a thing of it as she was, and started trying to figure out how many pages to skip in my lab notebook to allow for experiments I'd missed and would have to make up.

Zelda was setting out apparatus, not looking at me, but then she said in an odd, sort of choked voice, "If you'd like to talk about it any time, Liza, I'll be glad to listen."

I looked up then and when I saw her face the icicles started coming back to my stomach. "Thanks," I said carefully, "but I don't think so."

Her face seemed very serious, but her eyes didn't. "Liza, may I ask you something?"

"Sure," I said reluctantly.

"Well—I think you know me well enough to know this isn't out of any prurient interest or anything, right?"

The icicles in my stomach got colder; I shrugged, feeling trapped.

"Well," Zelda began, "since I'm going to be a doctor and all . . ."

It was at this point that I realized there were several other kids, mostly girls, but a few boys, too, clustered around our table, as if they were all suddenly coming over to borrow a test tube or ask a question—but there were too many of them for that.

Zelda went right on talking as if they weren't there, but I could see she was very aware of them. "I just wondered," she said smoothly, "if you could tell me, from a scientific standpoint, of course, just what it is that two girls *do* in bed . . ."

It did get better, although it took a while for some of the girls to sit next to me again in class. That was funny, in a way. At Foster we didn't have assigned seats, and as I said, I really didn't notice it in chemistry that first morning, but by afternoon it had become pretty obvious. When I realized what was going on, I purposely arrived a little late to my classes so I'd get to choose who to sit next to and could maybe show the girls that I wasn't going to rape them in the middle of math or something. I don't know; I'm probably exaggerating, but it did seem a little grim at first.

I guess if I add it all up, though, I'd have to say that for every kid who was rotten—and there were really only a few—there were at least two, like Valerie and all the kids who just said hi to me in an ordinary friendly way, who counteracted it. Mary Lou Dibbins, for instance, came up to me and said, "Thank God you're back—Angela can't even begin to stand up to Mrs. Poindexter at council meetings." There was a girl in history class who just smiled, came over to me, and as if nothing had happened asked if I had an extra pen. And then there was Conn, and what he told me.

It was later in the afternoon of that first day before I got around to reading the bulletin board in the main hall. A notice had gone up, dated noon, from Mrs. Poindexter, canceling the next two council meetings—which meant that, despite what Mary Lou had said, there'd probably only be one more I'd preside at, since finals were coming up soon. Seeing that notice was like having the last bad thing happen on one of those days when everything goes wrong. Conn came up to me when I was standing there and he obviously figured out what I was going through, which made it partly worse and partly better. "Life," he observed, looking at the bulletin board instead of at me, "is a crock of you-know-what, with all the wrong people falling into it. Still—you hear about Poindexter?"

"No," I said through the damp haze in front of my eyes. "What about her?"

"Leaving at the end of the year. Some order from the Board of Trustees. It's not around school yet, but there was this official-looking letter in the office that I just happened to see Baxter weeping over. Something about 'frequent demonstrations of poor judgment and overreaction to trivial incidents.' And 'continuous overextension of authority to the point of undermining democratic principles.' Also, you might like to know that Friday afternoon, Mr. Piccolo announced that the pledges are really starting to come in now." Conn put his hand on my arm, still looking at the bulletin board. "Liza," he said, "listen, MIT's going to be great, you know that, don't you?"

I managed a nod, and Conn patted my arm and said, "Don't forget it," and then he even had the tact to go away —and I still stood there. Right at that moment it didn't matter to me very much how good it was that Mrs. Poindexter was leaving. It did matter that it was obvious she'd been kicked out by the Board of Trustees, and that even though the disciplinary hearing was clearly not the only reason, it certainly must have been one of the reasons. The trouble was, all I could think was *I did that, too*—because right then I didn't want to have an effect on anyone's life, not even Mrs. Poindexter's. I just wanted to be as anonymous and unimportant as the newest freshman, from then till graduation.

But I decided, since this was my first and only free period that day, to go ahead with what I'd been on my way to do when I'd stopped at the bulletin board: go to the art studio to see Ms. Stevenson and find out how Ms. Widmer's and her hearing had gone—I didn't have English till last period, so I hadn't seen Ms. Widmer yet.

But there was a strange woman rummaging in Ms. Stevenson's supply cupboards. She looked up blankly when I went in, and said, "Yes? May I help you? I don't think there's a class here this period—is there?" The woman laughed in a friendly way as she went to Ms. Stevenson's drawing board and picked up a schedule. "I wonder how long it's going to take me to learn what's when . . . Is anything the matter?"

Ms. Stevenson's got another cold, I told myself as I ran out; she's just absent.

I think I ran all the way to Ms. Widmer's room. There was a class going on, but Sally was right outside the closed door, at the water fountain.

"If you're looking for Ms. Widmer," Sally said with a little smile, "I'm afraid you won't find her here."

"But she should be back today," I said, still stupidly bewildered. "The way I am. I mean, I got my notice Saturday, so she must've . . ."

"I'm sure she got hers Saturday, too, Liza," Sally said almost sympathetically. "That's why she's not here."

I think I said, "Oh, God," and started to walk away.

But Sally came after me.

"Liza," she said, "listen. You may not believe me, but—well, I'm sorry I had to do what I did. I'm sorry I was mad, too, and—well, I'd like to help you, Liza; Walt knows of this really good doctor, a shrink, I mean . . ."

I tried to brush her away and I probably said something terse like, "I don't need your help," but she hung on. All I could think of was getting to a phone and calling Ms. Stevenson and Ms. Widmer.

"Listen, Liza, the trustees had to do it, don't you see? Even if there hadn't been a fund-raising campaign going on, they'd have had to fire Ms. Stevenson and Ms. Widmer. Having teachers like that—it's sort of like my causing ear infections, isn't it? Only this is so very much worse. I mean, it just ruins people for—for getting married and having kids and having a normal, healthy sex life—and for just plain being happy and well-adjusted. The thing is—well, think of the influence teachers have." She smiled sadly. "Oh, Liza, think of yourself, think of how influenced you were by them! You always liked Ms. Stevenson especially; you almost idolize her . . ."

I swear it was all I could do not to shake her. "I do not idolize her!" I shouted. "I like them both—the way most other kids in this school do. I didn't even know they were —I mean, I didn't . . ." I sputtered for a few seconds more, thinking it might still be risky to say outright that they were gay. Instead I said, "Sally, I'd have been gay anyway, can't you understand that? I was gay before I knew anything about them." Then I heard myself saying, "I was probably always gay—you know I never liked boys that way . . ."

"Gay," Sally said softly. "Oh, Liza, what a sad word! What a terribly sad word. Ms. Baxter said that to me and she's right. Even with drugs and liquor and other problems like that, most of the words are more honestly negative— stoned, drunk out of one's mind . . ."

I think it was at that point that I did take hold of Sally's arm—not to shake her, but just to shut her up. I remember trying to keep my voice from breaking. "It's not a problem," I said. "It's not negative. Don't you know that it's love you're talking about? You're talking about how I feel about another human being and how she feels about me, not about some kind of disease you have to save us from."

Sally shook her head. "No, Liza. It isn't love, it's immature, like a crush, or a sort of mental problem, or—or maybe you're just scared of boys. I was too, sort of, before I knew Walt." She smiled, almost shyly. "I really was,

Liza, even if that sounds funny. But he's—he's so under-standing and—and, well, maybe you'll meet a boy like him someday and—and—oh, Liza, don't you want to be ready for that when it happens? A shrink could help you, Liza, I'm sure—why, they said at the hearing that . . ."

I stared at her. "Were you at the hearing?"

"Why, yes," she said, looking surprised. "At Ms. Ste-venson's and Ms. Widmer's. I thought you knew—I came in just as you and your parents were leaving. I was go-ing to speak at your part, too, but then they thought I shouldn't, since I'm in your class and we've been friends and all, and I agreed. But Mrs. Poindexter wanted me to talk about what kind of influence Ms. Stevenson and Ms. Widmer had on the students, on you, especially."

"And you said?"

"Well, I had to tell the truth, didn't I? I told them that you idolize them, because it's true, Liza. I don't care what you say, you certainly idolize Ms. Stevenson. And I said that maybe you thought that anything they did was fine and that you sort of—well, want to be like them and all . . ."

"Oh, God," I said. Running through my head . . .

It's snowing, Annie, Liza wrote—but the echo of Sally's words and of her own stalled thoughts interrupted: Running through my head—running through my head was . . . what?

She wrote again, groping:

The snow here on the campus is so white, so pure. Once when I was little—did I ever tell you this?—I saw a magazine picture of a terrible black and twisted shape, a little like an old-fashioned steam radiator, but with a head on it and stubby feet with claws. Someone, maybe my mother, said jokingly, "See, that's what you look like inside when you're bad." I never forgot it.

And that's what I've felt like inside since last spring.

Running through my head—running through my head now is . . .

Annie, if I'd been at their part of the hearing, I could have told the truth. I probably could have saved them— well, maybe saved them—if I'd been there. And even at my own hearing I might have been able to help them;

I could have said—I wanted to say—that they'd had no influence, that I'd have been gay anyway . . .

Liza put on her jacket; she went outside and stood on the deserted riverbank, watching the snow fall lazily into the Charles.

If I hadn't been gay, she thought as her mind cleared; if nothing had happened in that house, in that bedroom . . .

"But dammit," she said aloud, "you are gay, Liza, and something did happen in that house, and it happened because you love Annie in ways you wouldn't if you weren't gay. Liza, Liza Winthrop, you are gay."

Go on from that, Liza, she told herself, walking now. Climb that last mountain . . .

18

$\mathcal{J}$t comes back in clouds, in wispy images. I remember walking with Annie to Cobble Hill late in the afternoon of that first day back at school, the day Sally told me Ms. Stevenson and Ms. Widmer had been fired.

It was raining again; I remember that, too, and there was no one at home in the little house with the gardens front and back.

I remember Annie looking up at the doorway, saying, "I can't hate it, Liza, can you?" I didn't understand what she meant, so I asked her, and she said, "I've been afraid that I'd hate this house. But I can't. I love it. So much of what happened here was beautiful."

And Annie kissed me then, in the rain in the dark doorway.

The front door was open when we went back on Saturday and there were cardboard boxes all around and suitcases and Ms. Stevenson's "masterpiece" from the art studio was propped up in a corner, and the cats were in carrying cases so they wouldn't run outside in the confusion and get lost. The little house in Cobble Hill was being stripped of all the things that made it look warm and loved and lived in.

Ms. Widmer was out in the back garden, digging up a plant and obviously trying to look braver than she felt. Ms. Stevenson, in a pair of old jeans, was packing the last of their books. "Hi, you two," she said—she even smiled—when we came in.

What I did then was something I'll never regret: I hugged her. We held each other for a very long minute and then she pushed me away, smiling, and said, "Oh, look, it's not so bad. We're lucky. We have this place in the country—we were going to retire there anyway. I've been talking about doing some serious painting, and Kah —well, she's always wanted to have a big vegetable garden and some chickens, and to write poetry of her own instead of reading other people's. Now we can . . ."

"You're teachers!" I remember saying. "You're such good teachers, good for kids . . ."

"Well, we've had more than twenty years of that. Lots of people change careers these days."

But I looked at Annie and Annie looked at me and we both knew that what really mattered was that probably neither of those two brave and wonderful women would ever teach again.

Annie, today I went outside and in the snow in the courtyard outside my dorm I built a replica of my childhood monster and wished you were with me. My snow monster was pure and white and guiltless, and I looked at it, Annie, and it struck me that it can never turn black and ugly like the monster of my childhood, because what

228

is guiltless about it is what it is, not necessarily what it *does.* Even if sometimes what it does is bad, or cowardly, or foolish, it itself is still okay, not evil. It can be good, and brave, and wise, as long as it goes on trying.

And then, Annie, I tore the monster down, and wished *again that you were with me . . .*

*A*nnie and I went out that last Saturday to get lunch for all of us, roast beef sandwiches and Cokes. It was so much like an indoor picnic, among the boxes and the suitcases, that we all tried to be cheerful—but that only worked a little.

"I hope everyone likes roast beef," Annie said.

"Mmmmm." Ms. Stevenson bit into her sandwich. "Super!" She waved her sandwich at us. "Eat up, you two—oh, do stop looking like a couple of frightened rabbits. It'll be okay. There are a lot of unfair things in this world, and gay people certainly come in for their share of them —but so do lots of other people, and besides, it doesn't really matter. What matters is the truth of loving, of two people finding each other. That's what's important, and don't you forget it."

Annie smiled at me, and I felt her hand squeeze mine, and I think we both realized at the same time what a comfortable feeling it was to be able to sit there with other people like us, holding hands. But even so, I still felt crummy inside. "I—I know you're trying to make us feel better," I said, "but to think of you not—not being allowed to teach . . ."

Ms. Widmer stuffed a used napkin into a paper bag. "We should tell them, Isabelle," she said, "about when we were kids."

"When we were kids," said Ms. Stevenson, nodding, "and our parents found out about us—well, suspected— they told us we could never see each other again . . ."

"God!" said Annie.

"Yes, well of course we did anyway," said Ms. Widmer.

"We did a lot of sneaking around," said Ms. Stevenson, "for more than a year—it was rather horrible. And we got caught a few times—once almost the way you two did, as Kah very rightly reminded me when I was too angry to re- mind myself."

"So we know what that feels like," said Ms. Widmer softly. "How dirty it makes you feel at a time when you want to feel wonderful and do feel wonderful, new and pure and full of love, full of life . . ."

Ms. Stevenson got up and went to the window. Then she stooped and touched the orange cat's nose affectionately through the grating in his carrying case. "Look," she said quietly, "I can't lie to you and say that losing our jobs like this is easy. It isn't. But the point is that it'll be okay; we'll be okay. And we want to know that you will be, too."

Ms. Widmer leaned forward. "Isabelle was a WAC for a while," she said. "Between high school and college. Someone found some of my letters to her. Talk about In- quisitions—the army's a good deal better at them than Foster, I can assure you! But you know what? Even though Isabelle was discharged and even though it looked for a time as if no college would take her, one finally did, and after a while, once she'd gotten her first teaching job and held on to it for more than a year, it hardly mattered any more, not in a practical way, anyhow. And . . ." Ms. Widmer smiled lovingly at Ms. Stevenson. "The important thing is," she said, "that we got through that time, too, and we're still together."

Ms. Stevenson patted Ms. Widmer's hand, and then she came over to me and put her hands on my shoulders. "I should also tell you"—she glanced at Ms. Widmer, who nodded—"that Kah almost left me after my discharge. She went through more hell than I did, Liza, because she blamed herself for writing those letters to me—even though I was the one who'd left them around. She kept thinking that if she hadn't written them . . ."

". . . if I hadn't been gay," said Ms. Widmer softly.

". . . then nothing would have happened. No court-martial, no discharge . . ."

"It took me a couple of years to realize," said Ms. Widmer, "that it wasn't my fault—that it wasn't my homosexuality that had gotten Isabelle discharged, it was what people wrongly made of it."

Annie's hand tightened in mine and she whispered, "See?"

"I think," said Ms. Widmer, "that I had to accept I was gay before I could realize that it wasn't my fault about the discharge." She chuckled. "That's why I like that quote so much, the one about the truth making one free. It does, you know, whatever that truth is."

Ms. Stevenson—I know she said something then, but I can't quite remember the words.

I think I said something lame about their teaching jobs again.

And I can sort of remember the way Ms. Stevenson looked at me, as if she were trying to get inside my mind. She put her hands on my shoulders again, still looking at me the same way—looking right into me.

And she said—

Ms. Stevenson said—

"Liza, Liza, forget about our jobs; forget that for now. This is the thing to remember: the very worst thing for Kah and me would be to be separated from each other. Or to be so worn down, so guilt-ridden and torn apart, that we couldn't stay together. Anything else . . ."

"Anything else is just bad," said Ms. Widmer. "But no worse than bad. Bad things can always be overcome."

"You did nothing to us," Ms. Stevenson said gently.

"If you two remember nothing else from all this," Ms. Widmer said, "remember that. Please. Don't—don't punish yourselves for people's ignorant reactions to what we all are."

"Don't let ignorance win," said Ms. Stevenson. "Let love."

Liza pushed back her chair, her eyes going from the last part of her long fragmentary letter up to Annie's picture, remembering as the snow fell outside her window how the snow had fallen on the Promenade nearly a year earlier when they'd given each other the rings.

She looked at her watch; it was only six o'clock in California. Dinnertime.

I'm not going to think about it, she said to herself, getting up. I've thought enough already. I'm just going to go ahead and do it.

She found Annie's first letter from Berkeley and copied down the phone number of her dorm; she counted out all the change she had and borrowed four quarters from the girl across the hall. By the time she got to the phone booth on the first floor of her dorm, her mouth was dry and her heart was racing; she had to say "Annie Kenyon" twice to the woman—operator? student?—who answered impersonally at the other end.

And then there was Annie's voice, from thousands of miles away, saying with mild curiosity, "Hello?"

Liza closed her eyes. "Annie," she said. "Annie, it's Liza."

A pause.

Then: "*Liza?* Liza, oh, my God! Is it really you? Liza, where are you? I was just . . ."

"I—yes, it's me. I'm at MIT. I—Annie, I'm sorry I haven't written . . ." Liza heard herself laugh. "Oh, God, what a dumb thing to say! Annie—Annie—are you coming home for Christmas?"

A laugh—a slow, rich, full-of-delight laugh. "Of course I am. Liza—I don't believe this! This guy I know—he's from Boston, and there's someone in New York he wants to see. He just offered to switch plane tickets with me—I told him about us, a bit—he offered to switch plane tickets if I wanted to, well, try to see you. I said I didn't know, I'd have to think about it. Our vacation starts tomorrow. I—I was trying to work up the courage to call you. Liza—are you still there?"

"I—yes. Annie—sorry. I—I'm crying—it's so good to hear your voice again."

"I know, I'm crying, too."

"Switch tickets—please. We can go home together—my vacation doesn't start for a couple of days. I'll meet you at Logan Airport, just give me the flight number. Annie?"

"Yes?"

"Annie, Ms. Widmer was right. Remember—about the truth making one free? Annie—I'm free now. I love you. I love you so much!"

And in a near whisper: "I love you, too, Liza. Oh, God, I love you, too!"

A Conversation with
Nancy Garden

Kathleen T. Horning: When did you first know you were gay? How did you know?

Nancy Garden: It was a gradual process. When I was a child, I felt I was different from other girls in some way that I didn't understand. I wished I'd been born a boy, and as I got older, I was uncomfortable thinking of myself as a woman, or picturing myself married to a man. I had no interest in dating boys or going to dances with them. But I didn't know anything about homosexuality until I was in high school. I'm not sure of the sequence here, but around the time that a girl in the class ahead of mine and I were developing an intense, romantic friendship—we were falling in love, really—I read a magazine article about gay men; that was the first I'd heard about homosexuality. Not long afterward, my friend's mother found a letter I'd written to my friend and, based on that, said she thought I was a lesbian. When Sandy—my friend—told me, I thought back to that article, and suddenly my love for Sandy plus many incidents and feelings from my childhood and earlier adolescence fell into place; I realized that I was probably gay. That certainly made much more sense to me than being straight!

Both from the article and from Sandy's mother's reaction to the letter, I knew that gay wasn't a popular thing to be, but I didn't really mind the idea. As I said, it made sense. But despite all the clues I had, and the fact that I did pretty much identify as gay once I'd figured out that it seemed likely, I didn't completely accept it for a long time. I think I wanted some kind of mystical sign—God's voice booming "You're gay!" to me or something similar. Sandy and I spent a lot of time denying we were gay both to ourselves and to each other, even as we vowed eternal love, and kissed and touched. It was an odd and painful situation for both of us, being in love and feeling sure that was absolutely right. Even though I knew that being gay explained many of my feelings and actions in the past as well as in the present, even though I knew I loved Sandy, even though I didn't believe being gay was immoral or sick, and even though I didn't mind being different from most other girls, I still wanted some kind of definite proof. I don't know if that's because perhaps deep down inside I really *was* fighting it (I certainly didn't think I was) or if it's because I eventually did like a couple of young men and that confused me—but even so, dating them seemed unreal to me, a bit as if I was acting a part and trying to be "normal" after all. But always, from high school on, no matter who, male or female, was in my life, Sandy was the most important person in the world to me and the person I wanted to be with forever.

KTH: What were the times like for gays and lesbians when you were a teen yourself?

NG: Pretty bleak. I was a teen in the fifties, when most gay people were deep in the closet. Coming out was very risky; one could be expelled if one was in school or college; parents disowned their gay children or sent them to psychiatrists to be "cured"; gay adults could be fired from their jobs if they were found out or even just suspected of being gay. At best, homosexuality was seen as a mental illness; at worst, as something evil, immoral, or criminal. Any kid who was thought to be gay was of course given a hard time by other kids. No one knew the special meaning of the word *gay*, really, except gay people or people in the arts. *Fairy* for boys, *lezzie* for girls, and *queer* for both were the words I heard most often when I was growing up.

It wasn't long before Sandy's parents told her not to see me anymore outside of school; her mother considered me a "bad influence" as well as a lesbian. But Sandy and I were in love, and we went on seeing each other, and getting caught, and seeing each other again, and getting caught again. Her parents eventually threatened to send her to secretarial school instead of college if she went on seeing me, and even though luckily the head of our school assured Sandy, who's very bright, that she'd be able to go to college no matter what, that was still devastating. It was a terrible time, so painful that once when I was driving my mother's car with Sandy in it down a street that ended in a stone wall, I realized that if I drove the car into the wall, we might both be killed. Then we'd be together forever, I thought, and the terrible time we were living through would end. But I turned away from the wall in time, and I'm very glad I did, since Sandy and I, after alternating being together and apart for some years, finally got together permanently. And in 2004, because we live in Massachusetts, we were able to get legally married—after thirty-five years of living together.

KTH: Were you able to find any books or other information about being gay?

NG: Very few back in the fifties. And even just looking for books was scary, let alone buying them or taking them out of the library; what if someone saw? Encyclopedias said we were sick or immoral, doomed to loneliness and promiscuity. When I finally found the courage to look homosexuality up in a public library card catalog—no computers in those days—I did find a few adult books listed, but they were always unavailable. That was a subtle form of censorship, I'm pretty sure. Some adult books that were available then or a bit later—a few by Mary Renault, for example—contained characters who seemed to be gay, but that wasn't openly stated. Perhaps that was the only way publishers felt they could publish them, or that writers dared to write them. At the local bus station, I did find—when I was sure no one was looking—some cheap paperback novels whose titles and lurid covers made it clear they were about lesbians. Those books usually ended with the lesbian character dying in a car crash, being sent to a mental institution, or turning straight. But at last I found one book that did help me: Radclyffe Hall's *The Well of Loneliness*, published in England in the 1920s. It's about a very butch lesbian and covers much of her life from the time she's born. *The Well of Loneliness* was famous; it had been tried for obscenity in both England and the United States, and officially banned in England for many years. I devoured it (it's not a bit obscene, by the way), even though much of it is pretty melodramatic and it ends sadly. But at the end there's an impassioned plea for justice and understanding, and that made me vow to someday write a book about my people with a happy ending. *Annie on My Mind* was that book!

For a long time when I was a teen, there wasn't anyone I could talk to about being gay; it wasn't safe to do that. Sandy and I did talk to a few friends about not being allowed to see each other, but we didn't tell them we were in love, and it was pretty clear that most adults wouldn't understand. Looking back, I suspect a few would have, especially my own mother and the mother of a good friend of ours. But we felt we had to lie to protect ourselves and our relationship. When we were still in high school I did finally meet some gay people in summer stock—I was heavily involved in theater in those days. One of the gay people I met in stock was a boy my age, and I was able to talk to him. That was a great comfort!

KTH: How did you know he was gay?

NG: He and I came out to each other very late one night, and we sat in the back of the theater all night talking about ourselves and our feelings and our problems. He was the one who told me the special meaning of their word *gay*. I really don't remember how the conversation started, or how we recognized and trusted each other, but we did, easily. Back in those days some straight people believed gays had special ways of recognizing one another—a secret handshake, for example. But if there were such ways, which I strongly doubt, I sure didn't know about them! I did learn much later that gays would sometimes speak of being "on the committee" or "a friend of Dorothy" (a reference to *The Wizard of Oz*) as a way of indicating they were gay.

My friend told me about two or three other gay members of the theater company, and back at school, I suspected that a couple of my teachers were gay (years later I learned I was right). I think I must also have wondered about a couple of other kids, but I'm not sure I actually put that into words to myself at the time. How did I come to think these people might be gay? Perhaps it was because they didn't quite fit gender stereotypes—stronger in the fifties than today—of appearance, behavior, and interests, but that's not an accurate indication by any means. We come in all shapes and sizes and types, and only some of us are obvious.

KTH: How old were you when you told your parents you were gay?

NG: My mother died when I was twenty-one, and I never told her outright, although I wanted to and I'm sure I could have. She was a most wise and understanding woman, and we were very close. She knew what Sandy's mother thought, and she'd written a letter saying she didn't agree with keeping Sandy and me apart. (Unfortunately, that made things worse, but my mother's intentions were of the best.) I tried to give my mother hints that I was gay. I remember telling her that kissing a boy I was dating (reluctantly; for show and as a cover) was different from kissing Sandy. I think she said something like "Of course," but at the time I was pretty sure she didn't quite get that I was really trying to say that I liked kissing Sandy much better. I also remember standing in the door of my room facing my mother and singing along with the words of a popular song that had the word *gay* in it. I know she knew I'd read *The Well of Loneliness*. In fact, she told me she'd read it, too, but I don't think we discussed it in any detail, although I have a vague memory that she said she thought it was sad. I think she was waiting for me to confide in her, waiting out of respect for my privacy and for what I was going through.

I told my favorite aunt, my mother's sister, some time after my mother died and before I told my father. I didn't tell him till *Annie* was published, which wasn't till I was in my forties; I was afraid the truth would hurt him. I was also worried about his reaction because he wasn't someone who understood or was sympathetic to gays. But I didn't want him to learn it secondhand from a review of *Annie* or from someone he knew who'd read the book.

KTH: How did you tell him?

NG: I told both him and my stepmother one evening. I don't remember the words, except I referred to *Annie*, and to Sandy, and to my gay friend from summer stock. (He and I were still good friends, and my father knew him—at one point, during a time when Sandy and I were apart, my friend from stock and I had even talked about getting married. I told him the deal would be off, though, if Sandy came back to me.)

My stepmother had suspected all along, and she was fine about it, except she was worried about my father's reaction. He was very upset when I told him, and afraid that he and my mother had done something wrong in bringing me up—an understandable reaction, though a false one, that many parents have. My father was also upset because he'd always wanted grandchildren. Of course today that would be possible, but in those days gay couples rarely had children unless one of them had been in a straight marriage. My father loved Sandy, though, and that helped him get through learning I was gay. But after that first night, he always resisted talking about it. I guess he was in denial or trying to be, and I know he was deeply disappointed. For a long time he didn't display *Annie* with my other books, as if he was afraid someone might pick it up and see what it was about; it embarrassed him no end that he had a gay daughter. But he went on being warm and welcoming toward Sandy, and he and I did continue to have a relationship, although it was a difficult and complicated one. It had been that earlier, too, though, before I'd told him.

KTH: What inspired you to write *Annie on My Mind*?

NG: *The Well of Loneliness*. My own high school years. My desire to tell the truth about gay people—that we're not sick or evil; that we can and do fall in love and lead happy, healthy, productive lives.

KTH: What were the times like for gays and lesbians when you wrote *Annie on My Mind*?

NG: I wrote *Annie* in the late seventies–early eighties. Things were better, certainly, than they'd been in the fifties; the gay rights movement had come a long way by then, and the Stonewall riots in 1969 had made that movement stronger and more insistent, and our people less invisible.

But the climate for many kids wasn't much better than it had been in the fifties, even though the American Psychiatric Association and the American Psychological Association had said that homosexuality was not an illness. There were no gay-straight alliances, no hotlines for troubled gay and lesbian teens—in fact, not very many people realized or accepted that teenagers *could* be gay. Homosexuality in a teen was still seen by many or most lay people as a developmental stage or as "arrested development." Some adults, certainly more than back in the fifties, did know better, like the red-haired woman at the hearing at Liza's private school, but there were others who were more like Mrs. Poindexter and Ms. Baxter. Unfortunately, there still are.

KTH: Were there many books for teens with gay or lesbian characters when you were growing up or in the eighties?

NG: There weren't very many books written expressly for teens in the fifties anyway, not the way there are now, although there were lots of children's books. Most of the teen fiction around when I was in high school consisted of series like Nancy Drew and the Hardy Boys, or sports novels, or romances.

There were lots of teen books in the early eighties when *Annie* was published, but only a few that dealt with homosexuality; there weren't many gay books for adults either in comparison with today. There were a couple of popular plays, though, that Sandy and I read avidly when we were teens: *Tea and Sympathy*, in which a gay boy is finally seduced by a straight woman to prove to him that he's straight, too, and *The Children's Hour*, in which a lesbian who's secretly in love with another woman shoots herself when someone suspects the two women are lovers. But, of course, those plays hadn't been written for teens.

KTH: What were the books like?

NG: The first book for teens that dealt at all with homosexuality was the late John Donovan's *I'll Get There. It Better Be Worth the Trip*, published in 1969. There's a groundbreaking scene in that book in which Davy, the main character, and his best friend, Altschuler, are playing with Davy's dog, and suddenly the mood changes and the two boys kiss. It startles them and troubles their friendship for a while, but ultimately they decide not to worry about it, which was a very healthy attitude to be expressed in a young adult book at that time.

I'll Get There was followed by a few books in the seventies in which the gay character was usually an adult relative or a friend or classmate of the straight protagonist, and much of the story—if homosexuality was an issue—focused on how the straight protagonist adjusted to the gay character. In *Ruby* by Rosa Guy, published in 1976, there's what amounts to an explicit lesbian relationship between two girls. That was an important and daring first—I think it was also the first teen novel focused on gay characters of color—but the girls have no real gay consciousness; one doesn't get the impression that they're actually lesbians. In the few books that focused on relationships between teens that were more clearly acknowledged as homosexual, those relationships were almost always seen as developmental stages, or they ended with a breakup or death.

Sandra Scoppettone's *Happy Endings Are All Alike*, published two years after *Ruby*, was an important exception. *Happy Endings* was the first teen novel to have a clearly lesbian (or gay) main character; Scoppettone's lesbian protagonist is in love with another girl. But she is raped and beaten by a homophobic boy in a shattering, overpowering scene, and her lover breaks up with her because of it. At the very end, though, there is a hint that the girls may get back together. It's not quite a happy ending, but it is a hopeful one, and that, plus the clearly lesbian protagonist, made *Happy Endings* a real breakthrough book.

KTH: What's your opinion on the current state of gay literature for teens?

NG: I think today's gay literature is very healthy. There are some extremely talented new writers in the field now, some of whom seem especially committed to gay literature. And more publishers than ever before are bringing out books for teens showing gay and lesbian characters as a normal part of straight people's lives, as of course has been the case for a while in adult books as well. In addition to that, I've been especially glad to see that the trend at last now seems to be toward more gay and lesbian main characters. That's great, and I hope it continues! I also hope soon we'll be seeing transgender main characters, and more bisexual and questioning ones as well.

LGBTQ (lesbian, gay, bisexual, transgender, and questioning) kids are coming out at ever younger ages these days, and it's wonderful to see that there are now some younger teen and middle-grade books featuring them. Also wonderful is the fact that more books—novels now, as well as picture books—are being produced for kids with two moms or two dads—more books and better books! There are also a few for young kids that seek to counteract gender stereotypes.

An especially important development in many—perhaps most—of the new gay books for teens lies in the treatment of homosexuality itself, and that in turn both reflects and encourages what's going on among kids themselves. Many of today's LGBTQ teens eschew labels altogether or have developed more fluid or inclusive ones for themselves; many feel that it's "no big deal" to be gay or lesbian, bi or trans or questioning, or some combination of other-than-strictly-heterosexual. Many of them are proudly out and refusing to be seen as victims. Yes, LGBTQ kids still do encounter homophobia and ugly bullying and rejection, and all of those things hurt deeply; many LGBTQ kids do still have conflicts about coming out to themselves, their families, and their peers. But they are far less apt now than ever before to be defeated by these things when they do experience them. Their greater, stronger self-acceptance shows in many of the newer books. And that, both in literature and in life, is nothing short of beautiful!

KTH: What made *Annie* different from the other books that were available about gay teens twenty-five years ago?

NG: *Annie* was the first teen novel with both a young lesbian (or gay) protagonist and a definitely happy ending. In the same year as *Annie*, Aidan Chambers's *Dance on My Grave* was published—the first, I think, about a gay male protagonist and his lover. But his lover dies at the end.

In fairness, I should say that in addition to the fact that having unhappy endings was for years the only way authors could write about homosexuality and get published, I also think that showing homosexuals as victims was sometimes an attempt to demonstrate how cruelly gay people often were (and sometimes still are) treated, rather than a way of implying gay people were weak or deserving of punishment. I also think Scoppettone's book was the first to show a young lesbian trying to rise above homophobic treatment, rather than being destroyed by it. I was disappointed when I read it the first time, for the rape was so devastating it tended to overshadow the note of hope at the end. But nonetheless I was enormously encouraged by the fact that *Happy Endings* had a real lesbian main character.

KTH: How long did it take you to write *Annie?*

NG: In one way, I guess two to three years; in another, ten to fifteen or more. *Annie* had several predecessors. My first attempt, aside from agonized poems and some embarrassingly personal attempts at playwriting, was an adult novel called *For Us Also*. I started it in college and worked on it off and on for many years. Luckily, I never tried to have it published. Like *The Well of Loneliness*, *For Us Also* was melodramatic, and stylistically it was kind of a combination of *Well* and the Bible. At least it taught me a lot about how not to write a novel!

My next attempt was a young adult novel about two teenage girls who fall in love and realize that they're gay. It was called *Summerhut,* and I was thrilled when an editor expressed interest in it. But after I'd revised it for him a couple of times, he rejected it. Then I wrote *Good Moon Rising,* also a love and coming-out story about two young lesbians. That one had a theater setting. I didn't think the book worked, perhaps because I was writing about two things I cared deeply about—theater and being gay—and that's often difficult to do well. I put *Good Moon* away in a drawer and forgot about it till seven or eight years after Annie was published, when I revised and updated it. It was published in 1996.

One rainy day after putting *Good Moon* away, I was sitting in Sandy's and my kitchen having tomato soup for lunch, and the words "It's raining, Annie" popped into my head. I know it sounds weird, but something told me that at last this might be the beginning of *the* book, although I didn't know who was saying "It's raining" or who Annie was. But nevertheless that was how *Annie on My Mind* was born.

KTH: What was the hardest part about writing the story?

NG: Remembering to concentrate on telling a story instead of standing up on a soapbox and lecturing to my readers! I'd "soapboxed" a lot in *For Us Also* and in

Summerhut, for I was in a huge hurry to get my message across to readers. "Gay people are really nice," I wanted to shout; "we're not sick or evil or immoral, and we can fall in love just like straight people; it's cruel to victimize us or laugh at us or exclude us." But one can't say that kind of thing outright or force one's characters to say it if one is writing fiction!

KTH: Were any of the characters based on real people?

NG: Not directly. Most of the characters in all of my books are combinations of myself, people I've known or read about or observed, and people I've imagined. I think there's a lot of me in Liza, and there are bits and pieces of other people in some of the other characters in *Annie* as well, but no one's a carbon copy of anyone real.

KTH: Why didn't Ms. Widmer and Ms. Stevenson protest when they were fired?

NG: I think they didn't want to go through what that would have entailed. They'd already suffered through Ms. Stevenson's court-martial years earlier, and its aftermath. I think they just wanted to reconstruct their lives quietly, do some of the other things they'd always wanted to do, and live together in peace. And of course protesting their firing would probably have caused enough of a fuss to prevent their getting other teaching jobs if they ever wanted to go back to teaching. If they kept quiet about it and eventually applied for other jobs, it's conceivable that, given the climate of the times, Foster wouldn't admit to another school that they'd fired Widmer and Stevenson because they were gay. Few schools were willing in the eighties to admit they'd ever had lesbian or gay faculty members!

KTH: What do you think happened to Annie and Liza?

NG: I think they continued seeing each other whenever they could, and then moved in together after college. I imagine Annie's still singing and Liza's still designing buildings, and I bet they're still close to their families. Perhaps they're raising a couple of kids, too!

KTH: Did you have trouble getting the book published?

NG: Surprisingly, no! It was rejected by the same editor who'd rejected *Summerhut*; his was the first publishing house it went to. I balked at sending it to Farrar, Straus and Giroux (FSG), which by then had published *Fours Crossing*, the first book in my fantasy sequence. I told my then agent, Dorothy Markinko, that I didn't think FSG would want to publish a lesbian novel by someone who'd just written a fantasy. But Dorothy said "Nonsense," or words to that effect, and sent *Annie* off to FSG. Margaret Ferguson, my dear and enormously talented editor, who I think then was an assistant or associate editor, apparently was the first one at FSG to read it, and the story goes that she went running in to her boss and said, "We have to publish this book!" He agreed, and Margaret (who understood from the beginning exactly what I wanted to do in *Annie*) and I have gone on to do something like fourteen or fifteen books together.

My most recent book with Margaret, published this spring, is *Hear Us Out! Lesbian and Gay Stories of Struggle, Progress, and Hope*, 1950 *to the Present*. It's divided into sections, with each section representing a decade and containing two short stories. The stories are about lesbian and gay teens, and each section is introduced by an essay about lesbian and gay rights and issues in that decade. I've tried in both the stories and the essays to trace some of the changes that you and I talked about earlier, and especially to show the gradual transition over the years from our feeling and being seen as victims to our feeling and being seen as "gay and proud."

KTH: How did people react to *Annie* when the book was first published? ten years later? twenty years later?

NG: Much to my surprise and joy, *Annie* got mostly good reviews when it was first published. I was worried that it would be in trouble because of its subject matter, but almost every reaction I heard was positive. The first recorded challenge—the first request that it be removed from a library—wasn't until 1988 at a library in Portland, Oregon. (That's as far as I know. According to the American Library Association, there are four to five actual challenges and bannings for every one that's recorded.) I didn't hear about the Portland challenge, though, until some years later.

One of the really nice things that happened soon after *Annie* was published was that a reviewer told me she'd asked her sixteen-year-old daughter to read it, and although the girl at first had said, "Oh, Mom, I don't want to read about *those* people," after she'd read it she said, "Gee, they're just like any other girls!"

In the nineties, several more challenges were levied against *Annie*, including a big one, which I'll go into later. As far as I know, there haven't been any new challenges; I think there've been around seven recorded in all in addition to the big one.

Annie was on a number of "Best" lists in various years, starting from the time it was published, including the American Library Association's list of the 100 "Best of the Best" books for teens from 1966 to 1999. Back in the eighties, *Annie* was nominated for the Gay Book Award and for the Golden Kite Award, and it also got the Craberry Award, an award given by kids affiliated with a library in Acton, Connecticut. In 2002 it was designated as the 1982 "winner" of the "Retro Mock Printz

Award." Sarah Cornish and Patrick Jones, two experts on teen literature, solicited votes from librarians for one book per year of those published between 1979 and 1999 that should have gotten the Printz Award had it been in existence. (The real Michael L. Printz Award was established in 2000; it's the major annual award now for teen books.) The Mock Printz and the Craberry Award both especially tickle me!

Annie's been used in college classes about teen literature and about diversity, and just recently I've heard it's been used in a high school class or two as well. Over the years, it's been mentioned or featured in articles in magazines such as *School Library Journal*, *Booklist*, *VOYA*, and *Publishers Weekly*. The BBC did a radio version of it, and a man in Kansas, Kim Aaronson, adapted it for the stage with a little input from me. *Annie's* also been translated into several languages, including Chinese!

KTH: Did you get any letters from teens when the book first came out? Were they mostly gay and lesbian teens? Are there great differences in the concerns/reactions of straight, gay, or questioning teens?

NG: I got many letters when *Annie* first came out, from both teens and adults, and I still get them, although they're usually in e-mail form now. Most are from girls and women, both gay and straight, but there've been a few from boys and men, also both gay and straight. Most letters I get are from the U.S., but a few have been from other countries. The adult lesbians often say they wish *Annie* had been around when they first came out, or they tell me that they read it long ago when they themselves were questioning, or not long before they came out, or when they first came out, and that it helped them. Straight readers, male and female, have said that it's a love story that speaks to everyone, gay or straight, which is a really beautiful and very touching thing to say.

I've been told *Annie* kept at least one young lesbian from suicide, which makes me feel incredibly humble. Lesbian or questioning teens usually write about how *Annie* has helped them to feel less alone, to like themselves, to have hope; they say they identify strongly with the characters; some read it with their girlfriends or give it to their girlfriends; a few want to know if there's going to be a movie; most of them thank me for writing it. Often they tell me about their lives and sometimes they ask questions. I love being in touch with my readers (although some of them will tell you that I'm not the most prompt correspondent in the world!), and I've made many wonderful young friends through the letters and e-mails they write.

KTH: Did you get any hate mail?

NG: I got one hate letter soon after *Annie* was published; the writer quoted Matthew 18:6 to me this way:

"But whoever causes one of these little ones who believes in Me to stumble, it is better for him that a heavy millstone be hung around his neck, and that he be drowned in the depth of the sea." I kept that letter on my desk for weeks trying to figure out how to answer it, but finally I realized, as Sandy wisely said, that probably nothing I could say would change the writer's mind, so I put it away.

KTH: Has *Annie* ever been banned?

NG: Yes, in several schools, and it was burned on the steps of the building housing the Kansas City School Board! That whole saga—for it went on for a couple of years—happened eleven years after *Annie* was published. In 1993, unbeknownst to me, copies of the book were donated to forty-two schools in and around Kansas City in both Kansas and Missouri. Some schools kept the donations, some returned them, and a few removed copies that were already in their libraries. That led to cries of censorship—of banning. There was a lot of fuss in the papers and on radio talk shows, and eventually a group of extremely brave high school students and their parents from one of the towns involved, Olathe, Kansas, sued their school district and its superintendent for violating their First and Fourteenth Amendment rights. Eventually there was a trial, and the judge ruled that Annie had been "unconstitutionally removed" from the shelves of those school libraries, and ordered that it be returned.

That was a difficult and exciting time, one that taught me a lot. Sandy and I made three trips to Kansas City during it; the third time I testified at the trial. Librarians and teachers both in Kansas and Missouri and elsewhere lent their support to *Annie* and vouched for the book's value, and on our trips to Kansas, Sandy and I met many terrific people, especially the kids and parents who sued, and the local librarians who were risking their jobs to fight the removal of the book and who testified in court on its behalf.

KTH: If you were writing the book today, would it be different?

NG: Wow! That's an interesting question! If I were writing that very book today, I think its core—Annie and Liza and the love story—would still be the same. But other details would probably be a bit different. Would I have the teachers being fired and Liza threatened with expulsion? Possibly, depending on the specifics of the school involved. But I think I'd be more likely to include some other obstacle as I've done in other books. (Love stories, of course, always do have to have obstacles for the lovers to overcome!) Would Liza still be so worried about being gay? Maybe; maybe not. Fewer kids today are as worried as Liza was about that—but many still are. How worried Liza'd be would probably depend on where the book took place. If it still took place in New York, Liza might be pretty cool about being gay. In fact, she might be president of a gay-straight alliance at Foster Academy—or trying to form one.

I think the bottom line here is that the book would have to be somewhat different if I were writing it today—and that makes it even more amazing to me that it's still being read!

KTH: Why do you think people are still reading *Annie on My Mind* twenty-five years later?

NG: I may not be the best person to answer that question, but I guess it could be because most people enjoy a love story, and that, as I said, is *Annie*'s core; it really is a love story first and foremost. It's very gratifying to me that *Annie*'s still being read, for as you can imagine, that book has been hugely important to me, both as a writer and as a person. I feel lucky to have managed to write it, and grateful to Margaret for supporting it and helping me make it the book it became. I'm grateful to FSG for publishing it and standing behind it during those dark days in Kansas—and I'm more grateful than I can say to them for publishing this wonderful new edition of it.

Nancy Garden, whose awards include the Lambda Book Award and the Margaret A. Edwards Award, enjoys going to schools and conferences to talk to students, teachers, librarians, and others. She is the author of many books for children and young adults, including the picture book *Molly's Family* (with pictures by Sharon Wooding), the novels *Meeting Melanie* and *The Year They Burned the Books*, and a collection of short stories, *Hear Us Out! Lesbian and Gay Stories of Struggle, Progress, and Hope, 1950 to the Present*. Ms. Garden and her partner, with their dog and cats, divide their time between a small Massachusetts town and Mount Desert, Maine.

This interview was prepared by Kathleen T. Horning, Director of the Cooperative Children's Book Center, a library of the School of Education, University of Wisconsin—Madison.

COMMEMORATIVE EDITION

"If you don't put that ring on this minute, I'm going to take it back," Annie whispered in my ear. She leaned back, looking at me, her hands still on my shoulders, her eyes shining softly at me and snow falling, melting, on her nose. *"Buon Natale,"* she whispered, *"amore mio."*

"Merry Christmas, my love," I answered.

From the moment Liza Winthrop meets Annie Kenyon at the Metropolitan Museum of Art, she knows there is something special between them. But Liza never knew falling in love could be so wonderful . . . or so confusing.

No single work has done more for young adult LGBT fiction than this classic about two teenage girls who fall in love.
—*School Library Journal*

SQUARE FISH
NEW YORK · FIERCEREADS.COM

US $10.99 / CAN $14.50
ISBN 978-0-374-40011-8

9 780374 400118

99990